SAFETY IN BLUNDERS

The Worst Detective Ever, Book 3

By Christy Barritt

SAFETY IN BLUNDERS

CHRISTY BARRITT

SAFETY IN BLUNDERS

Season 1, Episode 3:
The case of the desperate and persistent
investigator
who just couldn't catch a break.

SAFETY IN BLUNDERS

CHAPTER 1

Zane Oakley hooked his arm through mine as we walked along the path, and for a moment I felt like Dorothy in *The Wizard of Oz*. I wondered who that would make Zane. The Cowardly Lion? No, Zane was fearless. The brainless Scarecrow? The heartless Tin Man? None of them seemed to fit my thrill-seeking neighbor.

We walked down a mix of gravel road and walking path through Nags Head Woods, a nature preserve in the Outer Banks, on one of his adventures. He was calling it *The Goat Man Project* and had chosen to record it using filmography similar to *The Blair Witch Project*. He wore a GoPro on his forehead, recording everything that happened on our daylong excursion.

"This is Zane Oakley signing on with my friend Joey Darling. We're here with the GMRO—also known as the Goat Man Researchers Organization. Now, the Goat Man is known to only come out at night," Zane said, whispering conspiracy-like. "So we probably won't find him. We're just looking for evidence of his existence."

"Hoofprints?" I suggested.

"Yes, like hoofprints. Stray hairs. A strange *baaing* sound."

"Or maybe a cashmere sweater or some tasty cheese." Zane cut me a confused look, and I shrugged. "What? That's the first thing that comes to mind when I think of goats."

"You sound glib now, my friend, but that will all change soon. The Goat Man is no laughing, cashmere sweater–wearing matter. He likes to chase people through these woods."

"As long as he doesn't kill them."

"He reserves that right for small woodland creatures." Zane lowered his voice and swung his head my way. "Or so they say."

I shivered and moved a little closer to Zane as the path narrowed. "Okay, that is a little creepy . . . especially when you say it in that voice. And how long has the Goat Man been said to haunt these woods?"

"Decades, basically. Teens come out here all the time to search for him."

"Well, it really is pretty here." I glanced around. With the exception of sand dunes, the Outer Banks was mostly flat. This nature preserve, however, must have been built on top of some centuries-old dunes. I nearly felt like I was in the mountains instead of a little stretch of islands off North Carolina's coast.

There were eight-foot drops on one side of the road and high hills on the other. In the distance, I could see where the foliage cleared and the Albemarle Sound began. I would have never imagined this area would be out here.

The good news was that it was nice outside today. Unseasonably warm for March. Warm enough that I'd worn a tank top for our hike, and I could feel the promise of summer on its way.

Zane crouched as he walked, reminding me of a character from *Scooby Doo* with his overblown sneakiness. There was no reason to be sneaky out here. We were the only ones hiking this lonely trail.

"What was that?" Zane froze and grabbed my arm. "Did you hear it?"

I halted, wishing I could say I wasn't scared. But part of me was. Because it was kind of creepy out here. And something shuffled in the woods not terribly far away.

My shoulders tightened. "A squirrel?"

"Too big to be a squirrel."

"A deer?"

"Sounded like a human to me. Maybe two of them."

The noise stopped. Instead of feeling better, the skin on my neck crawled even more. Was that a . . . moan?

No. It was just the breeze. Or a bird.

That was not the Goat Man. It wasn't. Because he wasn't real. Just like Bigfoot and the Loch Ness Monster weren't real.

Zane glanced over at me, his expression ultraserious, which didn't make me feel better. Then a smile cracked his face, and he elbowed me. "Just kidding. It was probably a deer."

I slapped his well-defined arm. "Not funny."

He snapped out of his melodrama and pointed to a road in the distance. "My granddad used to have a cabin over there. Hashtag: ohhowtheyearsgoby."

"People used to live out there?"

He sauntered at a normal pace now, dropping his act for a minute. "There used to be a village here, complete with schools, churches, and a store. Everyone headed out in the forties—probably because of the Goat Man. *Then* developers tried to turn this into another neighborhood during the boom of the 1970s. *Then* some conservatory groups purchased it. The people who already had homes here were grandfathered in, however."

The forest seemed to close in even tighter,

branches reaching for my arms. Algae-filled water from the ponds on either side of us crept closer, and roots felt like they were rising up. I'd always had a great imagination, which sometimes worked in my favor (e.g., acting) and sometimes didn't (e.g., right now).

"I don't know how I would like living back here," I said, glancing around for verification that something dangerous lurked close by. "I mean, I realize that we're not that far away from civilization. Still, it feels so isolated, like I've been dropped into the middle of nowhere."

"That's what some people like."

"I guess."

"The Goat Man likes it." Zane made a ghastly expression, and he raised his hands all supernatural-like.

"You said your granddad lived out here?"

Zane dropped his act. For now. "Yep. He built a canal from his house all the way out to the sound. When I was little, we'd take the boat out and go fishing."

I smiled as the image filled my mind. "That sounds really nice."

"When we weren't doing that, we sat on the porch and just looked out over the water. I'd drink lemonade and listen to his tales about life as a fisherman in this area. That would last all of fifteen minutes, and then I'd get restless and try to figure out a way to rig a zipline from the house to the water."

"That sounds like you. Adventurous and out of the box, even as a young boy."

"After we got tired of fishing and ziplining, my granddad made up stories about buried treasure here. My brother and I would search everywhere hoping to find it."

"What little kid wouldn't?"

"That is, until I ran into the Goat Man." His voice turned serious. "Then I never came out here to visit my granddad again."

I turned toward him sharply. "Really?"

A grin cracked his face. "No, of course not."

I elbowed him. "Zane Oakley, you should be ashamed of yourself."

In response, he hooked his arm around my neck and pulled me toward him. He planted a friendly kiss on my forehead.

That was right. *Friendly.* We were friends, even though he'd confessed that he liked me. I wasn't quite ready to return the sentiment, although at times I was very tempted. When it came to Zane, what was there not to like? He had a lean beach body, curly hair that was neatly trimmed at the sides, a contagious smile, and he was up for anything.

"Oh, Joey," he muttered. "What did I ever do without you?"

"I'm sure there are plenty of people who'd line up to go on one of these adventures with you." *Plenty of women.* I kept that silent. He had a steady stream of admirers.

"But there's no one like you."

"Flattery, my dear. I'm not supposed to like it . . . but I do. I really do."

"I know." Zane threw me over his shoulder and twirled me around.

I chuckled, feeling nearly giddy. The familiar scent of surfboard wax, saltwater, and coconut oil filled my senses. It was a pleasant combination that always made me want to drink in more.

I hadn't had this much fun since . . . well, since Zane took me go-carting. Or when he'd made me climb a lighthouse at sunset. Wherever Zane was, there was fun, and lots of it.

He set me down, and our gazes caught. I saw the longing in his eyes. He wanted to kiss me.

I'd seen the look plenty of times before.

And it would be so easy to get lost in Zane. To forget about my problems. To pretend my ex-husband hadn't crushed my self-worth. To imagine my father hadn't disappeared, possibly at the hands of an international crime ring. To stop trying to figure out if my future was in Hollywood or somewhere else.

But I couldn't forget those things. I needed to deal with my issues instead of falling back into my normal MO of covering my pain with the highs of stardom or with romance.

To break the moment, I poked Zane in the stomach and made a funny face. "You're a troublemaker. You know that, right?"

He shrugged and turned away, acting like our exchange hadn't affected him. And maybe it hadn't. I still couldn't read him at times. Part of me thought he was a womanizer. The other part thought maybe I could be the one to change him.

And that was never a healthy thought.

We began walking again. Searching for the Goat Man was one more thing on Zane's bucket list. And he was paid to document all his adventures as part of an endorsement deal with Slick Ocean, a surfboard company. He embodied their motto of "Life is an adventure."

He was living what he called "the good life." He did a little realty work, a little licensed massage-therapy work, and a little of this and that also. Mostly he grabbed whatever opportunities he could to surf and have fun while still making enough money to live.

"So when does the Castle and Beckett thing

start?" he asked.

It could have been my imagination, but tension seemed to stretch in his voice as he asked the question. Which was weird, since the whole Castle/Beckett thing was Zane's idea. Maybe he'd never thought I'd see it through to fruition or that the mayor would approve it.

I needed an "in" at the police station, and Zane had recommended that I ask the mayor to let me be an unofficial consultant as a part of my acting research. The mayor loved getting publicity for this area, and he used my fame to help him do that as often as possible. This was the one time I'd tried to use the situation to my advantage.

"Tomorrow," I said. "Everything has been done. Background check. Drug check. The mayor may have even looked into my history of fashion faux pas. I'm not sure."

He chuckled, but it faded quickly. "How often will this consulting be happening?"

"Once a week. I just have to figure out how to balance that and still pay my bills."

"After your movie comes out, you won't have to work quite so hard, will you?"

I shrugged. "I think you're underestimating the amount of debt I have. My life is representative of the house in *The Money Pit*."

"Bummer. I loved that scene where the bathtub fell through the floor."

I kicked a rock off the path and listened as it tumbled down a cliff. "That was a great scene. But speaking of money, I would have to say that it just made me miserable. It started to control my life and make me into someone I didn't want to be. All I want right now is to find my father."

I felt Zane's eyes as he glanced over at me. "No new leads?"

I shook my head, remembering all the events of the past couple months. I'd discovered some answers, but those answers had only led to more questions. "No. Nothing."

We continued down the wooded path, past little signs identifying wildlife, such as mosquito ferns and a devil's walking stick.

"What about your stalker fan club?" Zane asked. "Anything else from them?"

"Thank goodness, no." I'd thought I had only one stalker. Then I realized I had two. Then it came to light that I had a whole fan club of twisted little people who watched my every move.

So far they hadn't tried to harm me. But they did enjoy manipulating me in their efforts to keep my alter ego, Raven Remington, alive. They couldn't seem to handle both the fact that my TV show, *Relentless*, had been canceled and that I wasn't actually Raven Remington.

"Check out that cemetery over there." Zane pointed to some tombstones in the distance.

"Let's go closer," I told him, thankful to have something new to occupy my thoughts.

We trotted up the edge of the property, and I looked around, remembering for a moment those who had lived here decades and decades earlier. They'd been the true pioneers, living on this weathered sandbar without the ease of the technology we had today. Ease that offered plenty of advance notice for hurricanes that could put this whole place under water or winds that could send houses tumbling into the sea.

I paced around the perimeter, giving my respects. Then I stepped beyond the cemetery toward the stretch of water in the distance. It was like a treasure that we'd stumbled upon—a mostly untouched beach.

Serenity washed over me. Until I saw something I shouldn't.

"You've got to be kidding me," I muttered.

"What is it?" Zane asked.

I pointed at something sticking out from beneath some underbrush. "Is that a . . . mermaid tail?"

I felt silly even asking. I mean, mermaids

were just as real as the Goat Man or Bigfoot, right?

We crept closer. It had to be my eyes. I was seeing things.

That couldn't possibly be a mermaid tail because . . . mermaids weren't real, I reminded myself again.

But from a distance, it definitely looked like shimmery scales and a luminescent tail hiding beneath the brush. But it also looked empty . . . deflated . . . lifeless. Almost like a snake skin that had been shed.

By a mermaid.

"Zane, you didn't do this, did you? For ratings?" My voice shook.

"No way. I would have coordinated this better and called it the Mermaid Researchers Organization."

He had a point.

We stopped beside it, and I held my breath as I took a closer look.

"Whoa . . ." Zane muttered.

It was definitely a mermaid tail . . . and fresh blood was splattered across it.

CHAPTER 2

Detective Jackson Sullivan scowled at me, which was nothing new. Nothing new at all.

He stood at the perimeter of what the police considered a crime scene. He'd brought two other officers out here with him, and they were scouring the area for more clues and documenting anything suspicious.

"Did you touch anything?" Detective Sullivan asked me.

I shook my head. "Not this time."

Unfortunately, there had been a last time. It was a long story, but my heart had been in the right place. I promise.

"Throw up?" he asked.

"Nope." I'd fought off my nausea this time instead of spilling the contents of my stomach on a dead body. Or, in this case, a mermaid skin.

"Announce this to the press?"

That one got a scowl out of me. "Of course not."

But his look clearly told me that there was no

"of course not" in his mind. Probably because I'd accidentally done that not long ago. But in my defense, it wasn't totally my fault. I had been ambushed by that reporter.

"Tell me what you do know then," Jackson said.

As much as he drove me crazy, I had to admit there was something so very attractive about him when he was in detective mode. I mean, he was always handsome. No doubt about it. But he just seemed so strong, in control, and sure of himself in this professional role. It helped that his upper body was super defined, his five o'clock shadow begged to be stroked, and his green eyes reminded me of the ocean on a tempest day.

I remembered his question. *Tell me what you do know then.* So I did. With Zane's help, I recounted our walk through the woods leading up to this very unfortunate moment.

Jackson paused halfway through our recount and pointed to Zane's GoPro. "That thing better be off."

"Of course it is." Zane visibly cooled.

"We're going to want to see your footage, in case there are any clues."

"No problem."

"Great. Go on then. Did either of you hear

anything unusual?" Jackson asked, still holding his notepad and pen in his hands. Water shimmered behind him, a flock of ducks clacked overhead, and a kiteboarder soared with the wind in the distance.

Zane and I exchanged a glance. Just as Zane shook his head, I remembered something. Something that may not be important. But what if it was? My instincts were terrible on these kinds of things, worse than the casting director who'd decided Rosie O'Donnell should be Betty Rubble in *The Flintstones* movie.

"We did hear someone—or something— walking through the forest," I said.

"It was probably a deer," Zane corrected.

I shrugged. "It sounded too big to be a deer."

Zane and Jackson stared at me until I took a step back, halfway offended by their lack of confidence in me.

"Look, my dad was a hunter. I know a little something about the outdoors. I didn't say I liked tick-infested woods, but I'm not a dummy."

That seemed to appease both of them, and they didn't say anything else. *Take that!*

But as I stared at the mermaid tail another moment, a sense of unease washed over me. That blood . . . it didn't indicate good things.

"What do you think happened?" I asked.

I already knew Jackson's answer. Even if he knew something, he wouldn't tell me. But I had to try.

"It's too early for conjecture," he said.

Of course.

"Detective Sullivan, over here," one of the officers said.

Jackson maneuvered his way through the woods toward the man. I may or may not have followed ever so slightly behind him. And that may or may not have been out of pure nosiness.

I tried to look casual as I turned my ear toward the conversation.

"We found a purse," I heard the officer say.

"What's inside?"

"There's a driver's license. Cora Day. Says she's from Moyock. Twenty-one years old. There's also a receipt dated earlier today from the 7-Eleven up the road. Whatever happened here, it was recent."

"Provided that costume belonged to her," Jackson added.

I glanced back at the mermaid tail. This was a high-quality outfit, not something you bought at the party store for Halloween. Not only that, but this was an actual tail designed for swimming, not walking around in. If someone was wearing this, they would have to take it off to . . . oh, I don't know . . . *run away.*

The good news, I supposed, was that the amount of blood wasn't grandiose. It wasn't enough for me to immediately think the woman was dead.

But someone who paid this much for fake fins didn't just leave them behind.

And even though Zane thought those noises had been deer tracking through the woods, I had my doubts. What if we'd gotten here right as the crime was occurring? I shivered at the thought.

There had been two other cars in the parking lot when Zane and I pulled in. We hadn't seen anyone while out here, but this preserve had more than a thousand acres. Other people could be wandering these woods, and our paths may have never crossed.

I wasn't sure what had happened. But I didn't like it.

Nor did I have any reason to get involved.

Unlike the last two mysteries that had popped up in town, this one didn't have my name written all over it. That would greatly disappointment my stalkers, who wanted to reincarnate me as Raven Remington.

But the only mystery I wanted to solve was that of my father's disappearance. Not missing mermaids. Not the Battle of Los Angeles. Not even Amelia Earhart. Just my dad.

Jackson stomped back over. "We're done with you two—as soon as you hand over the GoPro."

Zane pulled it off and plopped it into Jackson's outstretched hand. "But I'll get this back?"

"Of course." Jackson nodded. "We'll be in touch if we have any more questions."

I nodded. "Sounds good. Whatever we can do."

"Ditto," Zane said.

Jackson stared at Zane a moment, his expression as unreadable as always. Finally, he said, "By the way, you've got some lipstick on your collar."

I glanced at Zane's shirt, and sure enough, there was a smear of pink lipstick. It must have happened when he picked me up and twirled me around.

"It's not what it looks like," I muttered.

Why did I even feel like I had to say that to Jackson? I didn't. I didn't owe him anything. And it certainly didn't matter whether he thought Zane and I were dating or not.

Zane took my arm and led me away. But all I could think about was that mermaid tail.

It didn't matter. I was walking away from this investigation and not looking back.

***

"Excuse me. I need your help with an investigation."

I paused from a little choreography number I was doing that included using my hair dryer as a gun while the James Bond soundtrack played in the background. I'd been blowing on the "barrel" when someone walked into Beach Combers, the salon where I worked part time. I was just a little bored.

I quickly put the hair dryer back into its holster—er, into the cubby on my station—and stared up at the man standing in the doorway. He was well built but not handsome per se. His face was too long and his hair prematurely thinning. His oversized hands almost made him look gangly.

I'd never seen the man before.

And what had he said? That he needed my help with an investigation?

I should change the sign outside from Beach Combers to Joey Darling, PI. Though I'd only played an investigator on TV, I couldn't convince people of that.

"I'm sorry—who are you?" I sounded confused, not demeaning . . . I hoped.

"Elrod Thomson."

"Why would you need my help, Elrod?" I patted the twirly chair across from me and motioned for him to sit. Dizzy—my boss and the salon owner—wasn't here this morning because she had a doctor's appointment. That meant that, for once, there was no Christmas music blaring from the overhead. In March. That was Dizzy for you. Unconventional. Unique. And delighting in it.

The man lowered himself across from me, his body language screaming distressed all the way from his slumped shoulders to the lines on his face. "It's my girlfriend. She's missing, and the police have marked me as a suspect."

"Is that right?" This seemed all too familiar. Familiar as in, didn't this just happen to me less than two months ago? "I'm so sorry to hear that. But I don't understand why you're here."

Haircuts and pampering could cheer up most women. However, I didn't think this man wanted an appointment.

He pulled his gaze up to mine, agony wafting from the depths of his brown eyes. "Because I saw you on TV—"

People got me confused with my alter ego all the time. I had to set him straight. "I'm sorry to break this to you, but I'm not really Raven

Remington—"

"On that ABC News interview. The one where you solved the murder of that woman's boyfriend."

Surprise washed over me. "Oh. *That* one." The one where I'd actually represented myself and not a fictional character. People had eaten it up and loved it. My manager loved it. Mayor Allen loved it. The piece screamed "feel-good TV." And who didn't like feel-good TV?

"Then I got a note—"

I stiffened. "A note? From who?"

"It was anonymous. But it said I should ask for your help."

My stalkers. It sounded just like them to send it. I shivered at the thought. They knew more than they ever should. Were in too many places. Liked controlling my life a little too much.

"I didn't know what else to do, and you really seemed to know what you were doing," the man continued. "And you seemed like the only one that cranky detective would listen to."

"Detective Sullivan?" Was there any other cranky detective out there? Not on my super-limited, nearly nonexistent radar.

Elrod frowned. "He's the one. He thinks I might have had something to do with my girlfriend's disappearance."

Realization washed over me, and facts clicked into place. "Wait—was your girlfriend the mermaid?"

He pressed his lips together, and his eyes widened. "You do have an inside track, don't you?"

I shook my head, needing to set him straight immediately. "No, I was at the preserve yesterday when I found the mermaid tail."

"You were there? Then it's a sign."

I shook my head again. This conversation was not going the way I wanted it to. "Let's not jump ahead of ourselves. I only stumbled upon it by accident." *As with most things in my life.*

"It doesn't matter to me if it was by accident or on purpose. I just need your help. I need to find her. I'm afraid she's in danger." He rubbed his hands on the glittery plastic upholstery of the chair. If he'd hoped to wipe away his sweaty palms, he was out of luck. These chairs repelled water like hydrophobic dust.

"I'm not sure what I can do to help." I had to be realistic here.

He reached into his pocket and thrust a picture in my hands. "This is Cora. I love her more than anything in this whole world. If something happened to her . . . I don't know what I'd do."

I glanced at her picture. Cora was a petite blonde with long, curly hair. She looked like someone who'd make a great mermaid. Innocent and happy and full of hope. And she had great abs, to boot.

I looked back at Elrod. "Why do the police think you're a suspect?"

He rubbed his temples, agony penetrating his gaze again. "Cora and I got into a fight. I said if she left, we were done. She left, told her friend about our conversation, her friend told the police, and now they think that it was a 'threat.'"

My chest tightened, and I lowered my voice. "Was it a threat, Elrod?"

"No! It wasn't a threat. I would never hurt her." Yet his voice escalated.

I knew about violent men. I didn't like them. At all.

I rubbed my arm and leaned back, putting more distance between us as I thought through my responses. I couldn't help an abuser, but I did want to help Cora. Before I could say anything, Elrod let out a deep breath and raked a hand through his hardly there hair.

"Look, I'm passionate," he said, his gaze pleading. "But I would never lay a hand on a woman. Really."

His voice cracked with emotion, and finally I

nodded. I believed him. For now. I reserved the right to change my mind.

"Okay, well, what about your fight then? What was it over?"

He sighed and rubbed the armrest again. "Cora was supposed to meet this photographer who'd offered to take her pictures. He promised her the world. Said he had all of these big-name connections and could make her famous. Cora fell for it. She thought he was the real deal and decided to meet him."

Something about that scenario left me with a very icky feeling in my gut. "Is that why she was at Nags Head Woods?"

"Yes, that's where the photo shoot was taking place. She loves it there, more than the beach even. She said she felt connected with nature and with the past. She always wanted me to go hiking with her, even when the rest of our friends were catching waves."

"Why a mermaid?"

"That's what she does. She started doing some local gigs—at aquariums and pools. She loved it. And she was good at it. She has this crazy vision of being the most famous mermaid ever. She wants to have her face in magazines and on TV. She's obsessed with fame and will do anything to achieve it. Anything."

Only two minutes ago, I'd been determined not to take this case. I wasn't a private investigator, no matter what anyone thought. But something about Cora's story captured me.

Maybe it was because I'd seen so many young starlets go to Hollywood searching for fame, only to end up being exploited and desperate. I was thankful I hadn't had to take that path. But I understood it, and I felt deeply for Cora's situation. Desperation could lead to awful things. Fantine from *Les Miserable* type of things.

Lexi Pennington's image flashed in my mind. She was a young woman who'd reached out to me in LA. She wanted me to help make her famous. Realistically speaking, there was nothing I could do. Also realistically speaking, I got requests like that all the time.

But I'd always remember Lexi because the police found her body two months after she'd first asked for my help. She'd turned to making naughty movies in order to make ends meet. Through that, she'd met some unscrupulous characters. That had ultimately led to her death.

I'd always wondered if I'd been there for her, if I'd listened to her more, if her story would have turned out differently. If she wouldn't have been taken advantage of. If I could have steered her in a different direction.

Lexi didn't have anyone to look out for her. That wasn't going to be the case for Cora. That was when I knew I couldn't say no, despite all my best yet not-so-great instincts.

CHAPTER 3

"What's on your mind?" Phoebe Waters asked.

Phoebe worked at Oh Buoy, the smoothie bar across the street from Beach Combers, and she'd become a good friend since I'd arrived in town. We weren't *Thelma and Louise* kind of friends. We were more like *The Odd Couple*. She was even keeled and as levelheaded as the plains, while I was oddly keeled and as levelheaded as a roller coaster. She reminded me a touch of the actress Kate Bosworth, with her wholesome good looks.

Phoebe only worked here in the winter when her dog-sitting/grooming/walking business was on hiatus. Oh Buoy, with its blend of nautical and tiki decorations, not only had awesome smoothies but also served killer salads and fish tacos—which was a delight when my diet allowed me to eat those things. I made sure it allowed me to do just that at least once a week. Maybe more, depending on my stress level.

"How do you always know when something is on my mind?" I asked, still reflecting on my conversation with Elrod.

She shrugged and slid into the booth across from me. It wasn't busy in here right now. "Good guess."

I played with the straw of my Coquina Crush smoothie and contemplated how much to say. I couldn't tell her that I'd actually taken this case. I reminded myself that this was my secret, and nothing good would come from sharing it. "You heard about the mermaid tail?"

"It's the talk of the town."

I chewed on my words before asking, "How much do you know?"

She shrugged. "Not much. I assume the police are looking for the girl. But that's another assumption. It could have been a boy with a mermaid tail. A merman?"

"Like *Herman the Merman*?" I smiled as I said the words, which probably looked odd, but I couldn't conceal my reaction.

"What?"

I attempted to snap out of my brief moment of bliss. "You never saw that movie? Not really surprising since it was pretty low budget and awful."

My ex had starred in it during his early days in Hollywood. It was such a humiliating film that I sometimes liked to watch it because the movie brought me a small touch of satisfaction.

Eric was supposed to make a comeback from that film in his role as *Captain Gorgeous*, but that movie had flopped as well, and he'd become a running joke on late-night television.

If Eric hadn't been so awful to me, I probably wouldn't have this reaction. And I wasn't proud that I delighted in someone else's failures. But I did, in this case.

"You seem bothered." Phoebe rested her elbows on the table, her attention on me like a psychologist talking to a deeply unstable client. "More bothered than usual."

"I usually look bothered?" Most people said I was too happy-go-lucky.

She shrugged. "Well, in your defense, you've had a lot of stuff going on lately."

I pushed my glib thoughts aside, reality crashing back down around me. I'd gotten distracted by the merman comment, but the truth was that a lot was at stake here. This was no time to gloat.

"I guess I've seen it so many times before," I told Phoebe. "Girls who would sell their souls for fame. Who would change their appearance to be called beautiful. Who would do whatever was asked of them for an unfilled promise. I guess in some ways, that could describe me. I did a lot of things I said I never would. I vowed not to let fame change me. But it was crazy to think I could do that. Of course fame would change me."

"As people, we all change all the time, whether it's because of fame or circumstances, hurts, disappointments . . . grief."

Her words clutched me. Phoebe knew about grief firsthand. Her sister had died of cancer three years ago. Claire had been married to Jackson.

"You're right. But people worship fame, you know? They hold it up as the highest pinnacle." I shook my head, unsure that someone as down to earth as Phoebe would understand. "I'm probably not making a lot of sense. I just really feel for this girl. What if she fell for a scheme and now her life is on the line?"

"So what are you going to do about it?"

"I don't know. I don't know what I can do." Although my mind raced with possibilities, all of which seemed outlandish. Search parties. A media blitz. A spot on *The Tonight Show*.

"You do a lot more than you think."

The past two months flashed back to me. "I've only solved mysteries in the past by accident. I don't even feel right taking credit for them."

"Maria Salvatore certainly thought you were worthy."

Maria Salvatore was an entertainment reporter with ABC News. She'd done a story on Jackson and me and had overinflated my role in the investigation. "She just likes a good story. Sensationalism at its finest. It made for good TV."

"I wouldn't be so sure about that. You risked your life for someone. That's pretty heroic."

I barely heard her. "Besides, what can I even do in a case like this?"

Realistically speaking, that was. Minus pleading for a spot on *The Tonight Show*.

"You use what you can to your advantage. Your main advantage would be your fame and popularity. What you see as a curse could very well be a blessing."

She had a point. The key to success was capitalizing on your strengths. Maybe I'd been looking at this from the wrong perspective. "Thanks, Phoebe. I appreciate that."

She shifted, and I knew the conversation was about to turn. "You excited about working with Jackson as a consultant, or whatever you're calling it?"

"The question should be: How much is Jackson dreading working with me?" Jackson and I couldn't see eye to eye on many things, especially when it came to police work. I got in his way. He saved my life. Lather. Rinse. Repeat.

I took a long sip of my smoothie, the fruity goodness euphoric on my taste buds.

"You really should give him more credit."

Oh, I gave him credit. He was a saint to put up with me. Or perhaps he was just obedient to his superiors. After all, Mayor Allen loved me. He was the one who'd kept me out of jail and who'd twisted Jackson's arm, allowing me to work with the police.

"I've only made his life miserable. Believe me. That's more than apparent." Replays of his scowls, his reprimands, his sheer disappointment filled my thoughts. Add some cheesy music, and I could have a Thursday night television drama on my hands.

"He just doesn't want to see you get hurt. He takes his oath to protect people very seriously. He's the type who plans everything. You throw him into a tailspin because you're so . . . unexpected."

She was being kind. I was impulsive and flighty, and all the good intentions in the world wouldn't make up for my often irrational actions any more than a new director had been able to ensure the newest *Fantastic Four* remake was a blockbuster.

"I suppose." I stood. "Well, it was fun chatting, as always."

"Come down and visit again sometime soon?" She lived on Hatteras Island, which was a thirty-minute drive from here on a breathtaking National Seashore.

"I'd love to."

"Next nice day we're going paddle boarding again."

"It's a deal."

I started to walk away, when Phoebe called to me again. I paused.

"And whatever you do, stay out of trouble." She smiled. "And give Jackson a chance."

***

I went home and did the next logical thing I could think of. Research.

How did I do research? By watching Episode 423 of *Relentless*. Of course.

Since Hollywood *never* got it wrong, I decided to watch the episode where Raven Remington discovered how someone was killed by examining blood spatter—and yes, that was *spatter* and not *splatter*. I'd made that mistake already. On camera. It was on the outtakes, if anyone wanted to watch.

With Zane by my side, I fast-forwarded to the part I was looking for and then pressed Play. I watched carefully as I—Raven Remington, I meant—came upon a body in a back alley. She began a monologue about blood spatter and what it meant and how to interpret it. It had been a bear to memorize. I'd stumbled and fumbled over those lines until I finally got them.

This is evidence of a blood droplet in flight. It possesses the shape of a sphere. If you look, the edges aren't smooth but have some scalloping from the force of gravity.

Based on what she'd said, I'd guess the blood spatter I'd seen on the mermaid tail was, indeed, not life threatening. It looked like it had dripped there from a secondary source. Maybe that wasn't comforting after all. But I hadn't seen any additional blood spatter. That didn't mean that Jackson hadn't found something.

I paused the show and leaned back on the couch.

"What do you think?" Zane popped a piece of popcorn into his mouth.

That was a great question. "I've got to figure out who that photographer was who took Cora's picture. I asked Elrod for his name, but he didn't know."

"How do you propose to find out who he was then?"

"That's a great question. I have no idea." I

paused, asking myself: What would Raven Remington do? And then I knew. "I could put out an ad seeking a mermaid photographer."

Zane froze with a piece of popcorn in midbite. "I'm rarely the voice of reason, I know—but I must say that sounds dangerous and risky. And are there actual mermaid photographers?"

"Good point." I tapped on my lip in thought, barely hearing him. "And I'm not quite ready to wear a mermaid outfit . . . unless maybe I do a juice cleanse. But it would still be a few days."

"Um . . . I don't know what to say. I think you'd look great in a mermaid tail . . . which sounds a little weird. Aside from that, you would definitely need some backup. Maybe a gun. And I don't even like guns. But you should really think this through. Besides, didn't you say your stalkers sent the boyfriend a note? Whenever those guys are involved, it's not good. They could be setting you up."

Lexi's image flashed in my mind again. "We don't have a lot of time, Zane. Someone could have grabbed this girl. Every minute she's missing is another moment she could die."

I'd stolen that line from Raven. But it was a good one. And it was true.

This was where I always struggled: Where to start. How to begin.

But this time I knew.

I had to head to the 7-Eleven, where the police had found a receipt in her purse.

CHAPTER 4

I had no cover story, and I should probably come up with one beforehand. The last time I'd decided to wing things when questioning someone, I'd ended up with the plot from *Men in Black*. It wasn't pretty. If I was going to draw on my vast movie database knowledge, I had to at least pick a movie that made sense with this situation and didn't involve aliens of some sort . . . right?

Yet the only interrogation scene that came to mind was from *Toy Story*, where the mean kid questioned Woody by shining a magnifying glass on him, thus scorching him with the intensified sun rays. I didn't really think that was a possibility as how to handle this. Now that I was really thinking about it—was that appropriate for a children's movie?

Thankfully, when Zane and I walked into the gas station/convenience store, Zane knew the man behind the register. There were advantages to small-town living, I supposed. I wouldn't have to use any magnifying glass—not that I had one.

"If it's not Dillan, my man." Zane raised his fist. "What's up?"

Dillan was in his late twenties with dark hair he wore long and curly. He had a lean body and an *I don't really care* style of dressing that included old jeans, a T-shirt with a rip in the belly, and some hemp necklaces.

Surfer, I decided. He screamed it.

"Getting through the shoulder season," he said, crossing his arms behind the counter.

I'd just recently learned that shoulder season was the period between peak and off-peak times here on the Banks.

Zane rested his hand on my arm. "Listen, my girl Joey here needs your help."

Dillan's gaze lit when he looked over at me. "What can I do for you, Joey? Any friend of Zane's is a friend of mine."

I offered my most winning smile—ask *People* magazine, and they'd agree—and held out a picture of Cora that Elrod had given me. "Did you, by chance, see this woman in here yesterday?"

He squinted and then nodded slowly. "Oh, yeah, yeah. The police came in here yesterday asking about her too. She must be the missing chick. Am I right?"

"You are correct." I leaned closer. "This is on the down low, but I actually have a personal connection with her. I'm trying to figure out what happened."

He raised his eyebrows as exaggerated understanding rolled over his features. "I totally get that. Yeah, I'll help in any way possible. However . . . I didn't see much. She came in here, bought some water and an umbrella stand holder."

"A what?" I hadn't intended on interrupting, but that was kind of weird and totally unexpected.

"I didn't ask any questions. People get them all the time in the summer. Obviously, it wasn't my business."

"Did she say anything?" I asked.

"No, but she looked a little nervous. She glanced around a lot."

It could be that she was nervous about her photo session. But what if there was more to it than that?

"What was she wearing?" I asked.

"Uh . . . a sweatshirt and yoga pants. I think she had something else on underneath. Something sparkly. Not that I was checking her out or anything."

I resisted an eye roll. "Is there anything else

you can tell us?"

He pursed his lips in another exaggerated expression: deep thought. "I guess I'll tell you what I told the police. When she went out to her car, there was a man on the sidewalk, waiting for her. They started talking. It looked heated."

My pulse spiked. Maybe that was just the clue I needed to get this investigation going. "Can you describe him?"

"That's the problem. I can't. I wasn't really paying attention. Not to him, at least." Dillan had the decency to blush. "Didn't think I needed to. All I remember is that he was wearing a baseball cap low over his face. He was probably in his twenties. Maybe early thirties."

Was it the photographer? Had he met her here at the convenience store for some reason? Or was there someone else Cora was having a squabble with?

"How about his vehicle?" Zane placed a lollipop on the counter and pulled out his wallet. "Did you notice anything about it?"

"Only because I looked at the security video with the detective in charge. But mud covered the license plate, so it's not going to be much help. I can tell you that it was a white pickup truck. One of the smaller kinds. Maybe an old Ford Ranger or something."

"Did he leave after Cora did?" I asked. Had this person followed her to Nags Head Woods?

Dillan shook his head. "No, he left before that. He stormed off like he was mad or something. Left her standing on the sidewalk."

Interesting. "Thanks for your help."

He winked. "Anytime."

CHAPTER 5

This was the day.

The day.

Yes, today I was participating in my first official ride-along with Jackson. Or was I acting as a consultant? Wouldn't Jackson love that? Either way, I still wasn't sure how this arrangement would shake out.

It was all part of my plan to try and gather more information about my dad's disappearance. Every lead I'd found had dried up. All I knew right now was that he'd discovered an international crime ring operating out of Shipwreck Bay Seafood in the neighboring fishing village of Wanchese.

My dad had connected with an international student worker from the Ukraine who had apparently discovered the dirty goings-on taking place there. The girl, Anastasia, had been murdered. Not long after that, my dad had disappeared. Numerous agencies were supposedly involved in trying to pinpoint what had happened to him. So far, it was all to no avail.

I parked at the police station and wandered inside, stopping by the front desk. I'd even worn one of my black suits so I could look professional. I was determined to sound that way also.

I'd considered doing an impression of Meryl Streep from *The Devil Wears Prada* but had decided she was a little too intense. Instead, I'd decided to go with my Olivia Benson impression from *Law and Order.* Warm but confident. Kind but determined. Stunning even into her fifties.

"Hi there," I told the woman at the front desk. "I'm here to see Detective Sullivan."

I had the voice down pat. Seriously. Not too high pitched. Not too low. Not too fast. Not too slow.

I was a living and breathing Dr. Seuss book at the moment.

The middle-aged woman's face lit up with delight. "Oh, Joey! It's so good to see you. Let me run and get him for you."

I frowned as she walked away. There'd been a hint of amusement beneath her greeting. Just what were people saying behind my back here at the station? Did they feel sorry for Jackson?

Most likely.

Did they think I was a joke?

Also most likely.

Did they resent the fact that the mayor had strong-armed them into doing this?

Also very likely.

I had a lot working against me here. But that wasn't going to stop me.

The Outer Banks was just a brief resting spot for me until I figured out my future. Was it back in Hollywood? Was it partly in Hollywood and partly somewhere else that would keep me grounded? Or should I leave Hollywood and its lures for good?

I didn't know yet. But as soon as I found my father, I'd be gone from this area. It was never supposed to be permanent. And I definitely didn't want to cut hair for the rest of my life. It was a noble calling . . . but not *my* calling.

I stood there in the lobby, pretending to study a map of the area that was posted on the wall. I'd tried to think everything through so I'd be prepared for today. I'd even done some juicing this morning, and now I had a water bottle full of green liquid in my purse, just in case I was tempted to eat a donut. Apparently, cops liked to do that.

Jackson opened a door into the office area. In an instant, I tried to read his shadowed expression. But I couldn't.

He nodded toward me. "Joey. Come on back."

He led me through a small maze of hallways until we reached his office. Then he pointed to a seat on the other side of his desk. I lowered myself there. Crossed my legs. Decided to uncross them and cross my ankles instead.

I wanted to study his desk. See what personal mementos he had here. Pictures. Awards. Anything that might give me a glimpse into what made him tick. But I had to stay focused right now.

He stared at me a long moment and let out a breath before saying anything. "So here we are."

"Here we are," I repeated, unsure what else to say. What would Olivia Benson say? No, no, I should pretend to be Richard Castle. And he would say something witty. But nothing witty came to mind. Maybe I should just stick with being Joey.

"You've been over all the ground rules?" Jackson asked, his expression still as unreadable as *War and Peace* was to someone with ADHD.

"I even signed them."

He steepled his hands together, and I felt like I was in the principal's office. "And I understand you'll be tweeting about this, as well as posting on social media?"

"That's right. The mayor thinks it will help

with publicity in the area." It still sounded strange to me, but who was I to argue?

"But you'll get our approval before posting anything?"

"Of course. I will use the utmost caution and reserve. They're my middle names. Joey Cautious-and-Reserved Darling."

His eyebrows flickered up ever so slightly. But I'd seen it. He was skeptical. As he should be.

"So what's on the agenda for today?" I asked, throwing in some innocently fluttered eyelashes for good measure. "I can't wait to get to work."

He straightened some folders on his desk. "Well, we'll be investigating a missing person's case."

"Cora Day?"

He twisted his head. "How did you know her name?"

Uh-oh. Think quick, Joey. Think quick. "Wasn't it on the news?"

"No, it wasn't. We haven't released the information to the media yet."

"Weird. I heard it somewhere."

He let out a skeptical "uh-huh" and pressed his lips together.

I shifted, reminding myself to be more careful. "Why haven't you released the information on her disappearance?"

"We've heard that Cora is a bit flighty, and some of her friends and coworkers think she may have taken off for Hollywood or New York."

"But the blood . . ."

"It's not definitive. She could have simply cut herself. Plus, she's taken off before. She thought she had a job down in Florida at one of the aquariums, but it didn't pan out."

"What about her family?" I continued, keeping my voice nearly as professional as my business suit.

"She aged out of the foster care system. No real family to speak of."

My heart pounded. She sounded like Lexi. There was something about broken people that drove them to seek the approval of the masses. To think fame would fix things and make their lives better. That couldn't be further from the truth.

"What else do you know about her?"

Jackson tapped a pen on his desk. "She was supposed to meet with a photographer, and we're trying to trace who this photographer is exactly. We looked at Cora's emails and text messages. However, the man she was meeting used an alias, as well as a burner phone. Beautifulphotoj@gmail.com doesn't tell us much. And Andre Delacroix doesn't exist."

"An alias? That doesn't sound good." Not good at all . . .

"Usually people's motives for concealing their identities mean trouble."

"Makes sense."

"He has a website, also registered under his alias," Jackson added.

"You've tried to call and email, I assume."

His eyebrows flickered upward with annoyance. "Of course. No response."

"So what's your next step then?"

"This is the nonglamourous side of detective work, I'm afraid. Since we've been unable to trace this guy's IP address or registration, I'm actually researching area photographers to see if we can find anyone who's a match to this Andre guy, who's set up dual identities perhaps."

Had he planned that specific boring course of action on purpose to discourage me? I wouldn't put it past him.

"So this photographer is your main suspect? Your principal lead? Your *numero uno* person to watch for?"

Jackson paused another moment, as if it went against every fiber of his being to share information on an active case with me. "He's a person of interest. Probably the last person she was seen with."

"Anyone else a person of interest?" Not me, for once. I was thankful for that.

Jackson pressed his lips together yet once again. This really was painful for him. "We're also looking into the boyfriend."

"Is it because the boyfriend is always a suspect?"

"The two of them had a pretty tense conversation before Cora left. He didn't want her to meet with this photographer, and he's apparently the jealous type."

"I see." I rubbed my hands—which were sweaty—on my pants. I felt like I should tell Jackson I'd met Elrod, but I couldn't. I knew how it would sound. "So we're staying in the office all day?"

I couldn't lie. That idea did not excite me. I wanted to be out in the field. I wanted to be in the middle of things. A small part of me wanted to be Raven. Just for now, at least. Until I had some answers.

"I'm not sure yet."

"I have an idea then." I rubbed my hands on my pants again.

A sparkle flicked in Jackson's eyes. "Let's hear it."

I remembered the awful, no good, very bad idea that I'd suggested to Zane last night. It suddenly seemed brilliant and like the perfect way to get out of this office. "We could lure the photographer out."

"How do you suggest we do that? We don't even know who he really is."

"We have someone pose as a wannabe model, offer this guy money for some pictures, and see if he bites."

"Interesting idea. Dangerous but interesting."

"It's only dangerous if you don't put the right boundaries in place first. With the proper planning and the right person—"

"It's not going to happen, Joey."

"Why not?" I felt halfway offended that he'd so easily dismissed me.

"There are other ways to draw this guy out."

"No, you need a goat."

"A goat?"

"Yes, like in *Jurassic Park*. The goat that lured the dinosaur out."

He did a quick headshake that clearly indicated I'd sent him into flabbergastion. Which wasn't a real word, but it should be.

"The dinosaur ended up devouring the goat, Joey."

I replayed that scene in my mind. *Daggonit*! He was right. "Minor detail. And it doesn't matter. I volunteer to be the goat."

"That's a terrible idea. The worst idea I've ever heard, for that matter."

"Who else do you have who wants to wear a mermaid outfit in March?" I didn't care what he said. I knew the answer: no one.

"If we were to do something like that—and that's a big if—we'd get Jenny to do it."

Jenny was the only female police officer here. "I've seen Jenny, and she's a lovely person. But I'd make a way better mermaid. I just need a couple of days to do a juice cleanse first so my abs will look good."

He stared at me. "You're serious?"

"Oh, for sure. Juice cleanses are very important—"

"I'm not talking about the juice cleanse, Joey." He blinked several times, as if holding back his annoyance.

I shifted. "Sure. I know if I did this that you guys wouldn't let anything happen to me."

He swung his head back and forth. "Putting a civilian out there is a terrible idea."

"What if I do it on my own?"

"That would also be a terrible idea. And you'd be charged with obstruction of justice. I could have you arrested."

"For setting up a modeling gig? That's ridiculous. Almost as ridiculous as George

Clooney's paycheck per movie, which could feed an entire third world country for a week."

"When you're in handcuffs, we'll see how ridiculous it is."

"What do handcuffs have to do with George Clooney's paycheck?"

Jackson started to correct me, when I smiled. "Just kidding."

"Of course."

I leaned back and crossed my arms. "I still think it's a good idea. I could pull this off. Who better to do it than an actress? Besides, we can't just sit around researching and comparing websites on a computer. A woman is missing. Her life could be in danger. We need search parties. Crusades. Candlelight vigils." *Tonight Show appearances.*

Jackson just gave me the look.

"I'm just trying to help."

He pressed his lips together. "You do realize we didn't bring you on to help. We brought you on to observe."

Ouch! "I'm pretty sure the mayor said to consult."

"Consultants bring a certain set of expertise to the table."

Double ouch! "And my area of expertise is acting. So there's your answer. This is why I'm here."

He chuckled—not in an amused way but in a dumbfounded one—and ran a hand over his face. "You're a piece of work, Joey Darling. I can tell you that."

"I've never been a hundred percent sure what that means, but I'll just assume it's a compliment and say thank you." I stared at him. "So do you want me to email this photographer or not?"

***

In the matter of an hour, I'd gotten in contact with one of my old Hollywood friends who was an expert in Photoshop. He could make me look ten pounds lighter with just a few strokes on his keyboard. He was a miracle worker. His talents made me feel slightly guilty, considering people's body-image issues and the rightfully unreachable standards of beauty in Hollywood, but that was a battle and discussion for another day. Today, the alterations worked in my favor and for the good of humanity.

Today, in ten minutes flat, Moon Zowie—yes, that was the moniker my Photoshop miracle worker went by—transposed my head to the body of a mermaid impersonator.

He'd also changed just enough of my facial

features that I wouldn't be instantly recognizable. He'd made my face a little longer, my eyes a little farther apart, and my lips a little plumper. Then he'd sent me the image.

I showed Jackson my phone.

"Not bad," he muttered.

That might be the closest he got to giving a compliment. I wasn't sure.

I was careful before asking my next question. "So what do you think?"

"What's your alias going to be?" Jackson asked.

"Ari White." Ari was short for Ariel. Of course. Was there any other name for a mermaid? "I've already set up a fake email."

"You're better at this than I thought."

"There was a time I had to dodge paparazzi by pulling stunts like this. It's all good." I'd worn disguises, made reservations under fake names, rode in discreet cars. I'd had to be like that, since the paparazzi were brutal. Who knew those skills would come in handy now?

"What makes you so sure he'll fall for your email and not ours?" Jackson asked.

"You probably sounded like the police."

He made a face. "Of course we didn't."

I made a face back. "Let me read it."

He let out a sigh but, surprisingly, pulled

something up on his computer. He turned the screen toward me, and I read the words there.

"Hi, I'd totally love a photo session," I read aloud. "Can we meet? Love your photos." I looked up at Jackson. "This screams law enforcement. Maybe I can give you guys some acting classes."

Jackson stared at me another moment. "Okay, send him the email you wrote, and see if there's a response. If this Andre guy is behind the disappearance of Cora, he may not be interested in coming out of hiding."

"You mean, if he's a predator?" The word actually gave me a chill.

"Exactly. I hope you understand what you're getting yourself into."

Of course I had no idea, but I hit Send anyway. I'd already typed up the message, crossing my fingers that I might get a response.

Hello. My name is Ari White, but I'm also known as the White Mermaid. I want more than anything to be discovered and do this full time so I can not only do what I love, but also work to save marine life as well. The ocean is like a second home to me, and I care for the creatures there as if they are my people. I saw your portfolio and think you're ah-mazing. Can we please set up an appointment so my dreams can come true? ASAP, preferably, as a talent scout is wanting to meet me this weekend. I'll pay double. Peace out. Ari White.

Thirty minutes after I sent the email, my phone buzzed. I glanced down at the screen, and my eyes widened with surprise. "He emailed me back."

"Who did?"

"The photographer. The supposed Andre Delacroix."

"Well, what did he say?"

My hands trembled slightly as I looked down at the email.

"He said he can meet. Tomorrow."

CHAPTER 6

Police Chief Lawson stared at Jackson and me after we told him how quickly things had unfolded.

The truth was, I didn't know much about the man. He was a quiet presence, hands off unless he needed to be hands on. He seemed to run things behind the scenes, only stepping into the limelight when necessary. All in all, he seemed honorable. Now that I knew he hadn't hurt my dad.

He was in his fifties, on the shorter side, with gray hair he kept short. His head was a pleasant oval shape, and the skin across his face was amazingly tight and unwrinkled for someone with a stressful job.

"You can do this," Chief Lawson finally said. "But I insist that Jackson is with you."

"You mean as a bodyguard? In the woods? Hiding?" More outlandish things rushed through my thoughts, things like undercover snorkeling operatives. Agents buried in the sand breathing through a straw. Parasailing watchdogs parading as tourists.

I'd been in Hollywood too long.

Thankfully, I'd kept those thoughts silent.

The chief shook his head. "No, he's going to be your boyfriend."

I froze in my little padded seat. "My boyfriend? Is that necessary? I mean, this guy may not want to meet if I have someone with me. He seems squirrelly."

"It's a risk we're going to have to take," Chief Lawson continued, his hands on his hips. "I can't send you out there alone. It's not wise and too much of a liability, even with a waiver."

Jackson remained unusually quiet, letting the chief fight this battle.

"But—"

"Put a cover story together," he continued. "And we'll set some ground rules."

"Understood." I could tell by his voice that there was no room for argument. If I pushed too much, he'd pull me off the case altogether.

"We've got to find this girl," the chief said. "I'm sure you both know the statistics about her odds of being found alive decreasing as more time goes by. They're not good. We're also going to need to talk about location. We can't do the preserve again. It's too obvious. I have someone working on that." He paused and looked at me. "Can you handle this?"

"Me? Yeah, I can totally handle this. Acting is what I do. It's Jackson I'm worried about."

"You're worried about me?" Jackson's lips parted in surprise. "Really?"

"I mean, can you act?"

"This isn't my first rodeo, Joey."

I raised my hands. "I didn't say it was. I just have a hard time picturing you pretending to be someone you're not."

"I assume you two will work this out?" Chief Lawson asked.

"Of course," Jackson and I said at the same time. Jackson said it with a dull, no-nonsense voice. I said it with a little too much enthusiasm.

Either way, the chief stared at both of us before finally nodding. "Okay, let's do this."

Awkward silence fell between Jackson and me as soon as the chief left.

I was the one to break the quiet. "So . . . I guess we need to talk."

"I guess we do." He pressed his lips together and grabbed his keys. "While you're thinking, I've got to run home and let Ripley out. Do you want to come?"

My heart leapt into my throat. The reaction

was irrational. I knew that. But I'd never seen Jackson's place. I had no idea where he lived. If he had a house or an apartment or camper. I wanted to know if he was a slob or if he was neat. If he had sports posters posing as decorations and furniture that used to belong to his grandmother.

But I was way more excited than I should be.

"Sure," I said, trying to sound casual. "I'll come."

"Great. We can rehash some things while we're there."

***

My awareness of Jackson was way more than I wanted it to be as we rode to his house. I shouldn't feel anything. I had no reason to.

But I did. Like it or not, I was excited. So excited that I rambled on and on about the best detoxes. I'd mostly wanted to pass the time without awkward silence, so I decided to make awkward conversation instead.

Finally, we pulled to a stop in front of a little cottage not terribly far from Jockey's Ridge, a giant sand dune and state park where people skydived and flew kites.

His house was small, up on stilts—but not

incredibly high stilts, like some homes in the area—and clearly showed that the person living here liked to spend time on the water. There was a fish-cleaning station, weathered buoys hanging on the wall, and a small boat beneath the house.

It fit Jackson. I didn't know what I was expecting, but this was pretty close to what I'd imagined.

"You like to fish?" I asked, not surprised.

"When I can."

"It's been a long time since I went fishing. My dad and I used to go."

Jackson stole a glance at me as we moved toward the door. "I just can't see you fishing."

"Well, I can."

"Next time I go out, I'm going to call you so you can prove it."

"It's a deal."

"You've got to put a worm on the hook though."

"You're not scaring me." Okay, I actually hated those squirming, wiggling little creepy crawlies. But I'd done it before, and I could do it again.

As soon as I walked into his house, I didn't even have time to soak anything in. No, Ripley greeted me with circles and tail wags and playful barks. The rambunctious Australian shepherd always knew how to make me feel loved.

I stooped down and rubbed his head, talking in soothing doggy tones to his very attentive, always adorable face.

"Why do you love that dog so much?" Jackson asked, dropping his keys on the table.

I stood and shrugged, one hand still patting Ripley's head. "I don't know. Unconditional love, I guess. What's there not to crave about that?"

Unconditional love was like a foreign concept in my world. My dad had been the only one who'd really loved me like that. Not even my mom had loved me enough to stay around. Most of my friends had disappeared when my marriage fell apart and my career seemed to sink.

Most of the time I felt utterly alone in the world, and I hated that feeling. I hated it.

"I think Ripley likes you better than he likes me," Jackson said, shaking his head at the canine.

"I'm sure that's not true." I gave the dog one more pat and then straightened. I glanced around, trying not to be too obvious. At first glance, I soaked in the worn leather couch, the faded driftwood-hewn floors, the stone-faced fireplace. "Nice place."

Jackson walked toward the back, undoing the top button of his olive-colored shirt. "Thanks. It's not fancy, but it gets me through. Let me put Ripley in the backyard. Feel free to grab a drink from the fridge."

"Got it." I waited until Jackson and Ripley were outside before wandering into the kitchen, opening the fridge, and pulling out a water. I quickly noted that Jackson had a decent selection of leftovers. Closing my eyes, I pictured him cooking in this space. The image was just a little too appealing. A *lot* too appealing.

I twisted the cap off and took a long sip to cool off.

Just as I put the bottle onto the counter, Jackson strode back inside.

"As we wait on Ripley, let's talk about tomorrow," Jackson said, pausing beside me.

"First, I should order a costume, right?"

"I have another idea, but we should look, as a backup plan."

"If someone is paying good money to have these photos done, they're going to have a decent costume. My whole cover will be blown if I show up and don't look legit."

"Let's make sure you look legit then." He walked across the room and brought his laptop over to the breakfast bar.

Then he stood behind me—a little too close for comfort—as I searched through the various sites.

"For the record, I still don't like this," he muttered, his breath ruffling my hair.

Tingles burst up and down my spine. "For the record, I know. But just let me do something selfless for once. Most of my life I've lived for myself. It's time I do something for others."

"I'd say you've done plenty."

"And I'd say I've left a trail of destruction in my path." I cleared my throat, trying to halt my thoughts before they began to pummel me. I pointed to a costume. "Check out this one."

"It could work. Keep it in mind. It's not cheap, is it?" Jackson leered at the price. "More than three thousand dollars. That's insane. Can we rent one?"

"The question is: Can we rent one that looks legit?"

Jackson and I both stared at the screen. I leaned back ever so slightly, trying to think this all through. So many things could go wrong, but it was a chance I had to take. For Lexi's sake.

"You're rubbing your scar again."

Jackson's low voice pulled me from my thoughts.

I looked down at my hand. Sure enough, I was touching the very area where a broken vase had cut me when Eric pushed me down the stairs.

"Habit, I guess."

"You do that whenever you're feeling anxious."

My throat tightened, and I forced myself not to look at Jackson. I was all too aware of his body heat next to me. Of the scent of his spicy cologne. Of how the man simply exuded masculinity in a way that was very appealing. Why did he have to notice how I constantly touched the reminder of my past mistakes?

"Do I?" My throat hurt as I asked the question.

"Just an observation."

Finally, I turned around. It was just as I feared—anticipated, hoped for, wanted? Jackson was close enough that I could easily reach up and touch him.

"My father risked his life." My voice sounded raspy with emotion as my gaze connected with his. "It's the most selfless thing a person can do for another."

I shoved a hair behind my ear, wishing I didn't feel so antsy. Wishing Jackson didn't have this effect on me. Wishing men weren't my weakness.

Jackson's anguished gaze latched on to mine. "Your father is missing now."

"You'll be beside me. With me. It will all be

fine." I drew in a deep breath, trying not to dwell on everything that could go wrong. "Speaking of which, let's talk about the cover story. What do you think of this? I thought I'd stick as close to the truth as possible. We met when you came into my salon for a haircut. It was love at first sight." At once, I realized what I said and flinched. "That part isn't close to the truth. Of course."

His gaze was intense on mine. So intense that I couldn't think straight. All I wanted to do was stare into his eyes. Reach out and touch him.

He didn't say anything. I pressed my hands behind me on the counter, desperate to keep them still, and wondered why he was so quiet. What was he thinking? That I was a nut?

"Well?" I finally asked.

The moment broke as he looked away. He reached across the counter and grabbed the coffeepot. "It sounds good."

I let out a mental sigh of relief. And then I fell back into my natural defense mechanism: humor. "And I was thinking your name could be Sheldon."

"Sheldon?" He glanced back and raised an eyebrow as he scooped grounds into a filter.

"Yeah, and you work for animal control. That way when you give off the law enforcement vibe, it will make sense."

"I see." He actually sounded amused as he pushed the On button and turned his attention back to me.

I swallowed, my throat tight. How was I ever going to pretend he was my boyfriend? I was an actress. This was my jam. Yet something about Jackson threw me all off balance.

"You and me, huh?" He reached up and brushed a hair away from my face.

I sucked in a breath.

"You can't look like that, Joey," Jackson murmured.

I closed my eyes, wanting to ignore all the warm fuzzy feelings having a party inside my gut and my bloodstream and my heart. "Like what?"

"Like you want to run."

The warm fuzzies cooled quickly, and I opened my eyes. "What do you mean?"

"I'm supposed to be your boyfriend, and you look horrified."

I snorted, the party inside me ending with an abrupt unplugging of the music. "I'm not horrified."

"Could have fooled me."

"I'm just not in acting mode yet. It will take me a while to get into character."

"Of course."

"No, really. I had an acting coach for years. Yanic. He was ah-mazing. We met before every episode of *Relentless*, and he helped me get into character. Acting isn't as easy as you think."

When someone knocked on the door, Jackson stepped back and smiled.

"Special delivery."

A woman I'd never seen before stood at the door holding a . . . mermaid costume? She handed it off to him, they exchanged some indecipherable words, and then she was gone, leaving Jackson holding the . . . dry-cleaning bag?

"I didn't want to mention this in case it didn't work out," Jackson said, walking back toward me. "But a lady at church has a daughter who likes to pretend to be a mermaid. I asked if we might borrow the costume for something."

"How old is this daughter? Please don't say eight, because there's no way I'm going to fit."

"She's sixteen."

"Let's hope I still have my youthful figure." I jutted a hip out and ran a hand down my silhouette, just being silly.

"I'd say you do."

Something about Jackson's words made heat rush to my cheeks. I didn't even think he'd meant to make that happen. Yet there was still a part of me that held on to my modesty, just as I'd been raised to do. All my years in Hollywood had changed many things, but glimpses of my old value system were still present in my core. I was working to strengthen them.

Jackson handed the bag to me. "Why don't you go try it out?"

I stared at him. "Now?"

He twisted his head in confusion. "Is there a better time? You're meeting the photographer tomorrow."

A million excuses ran through my mind. Excuses about not being ready—physically or mentally—to wear this in public. Yet it wasn't in public. It was just around Jackson. Which in some ways seemed worse than wearing it in public.

"We need to make sure it will work for you," Jackson continued. "If you're more comfortable, we can do this down at the police station."

I waved a hand in the air. "Oh, no. Of course not. I'm fine doing it here."

Who wouldn't want to wear a mermaid tail around an incredibly handsome man who thought she was a fruitcake?

"I'll just . . . uh, go back here and see if it fits."

"You want to use the spare bedroom?" Jackson asked, following behind me.

What I really wanted was for him not to be quite as close to me right now. Because

something weird was happening inside my brain
. . . I felt flustered and nervous, for some reason.
Hundreds of men wanted to date me—to date
the person they thought I was. And one small-
town detective made me feel like the most
inexperienced amateur on the planet.

"Yeah, that sounds great."

He opened a door at the end of the hallway
and stepped inside a spare bedroom. My gaze
scanned it. The room was pretty masculine.
Double bed with a navy-blue comforter. Plain
wooden dresser. No knickknacks or pictures.

At once, I realized he'd probably never lived
here with Claire. There was absolutely no
woman's touch at this place.

"It's all yours," Jackson said.

"Excellent." I slipped inside and, for good
measure, locked the door. I wasn't sure why I
did. It wasn't because I didn't trust Jackson. I just
felt safer this way.

I stared at the sparkly mermaid costume.
Shimmery blue-and-green scales. A lovely
translucent tail with extravagant scallops. Fairly
full-coverage bikini top with matching scales. It
was surprisingly heavy and made from silicon.

This was going to be horrible, I realized. Flat-
out horrible. A terrible idea.

But I was in too deep now. Deep enough that

if I came up too fast I could get the bends.

I took a deep breath and jumped into the task, taking my business suit off and replacing it with this hideous mermaid costume. The last thing I pulled on was the tail. I had to sit on the bed to do so and carefully slip each leg inside what felt like a giant blood pressure cuff. I hoped I didn't look like a stuffed sausage link in this thing.

When I'd pulled the outfit up to my waist, I tried to stand and nearly fell on the floor. It was like walking with your ankles tied together . . . and an invisible trip line attached. Could I move while remaining upright in this thing? I wasn't sure. But I knew Jackson had to see this. He had to give his stamp of approval that I wasn't going to blow this whole sting.

I considered my options. I could do a mermaid pose—either on my side or on my belly with my tail raised. There was no room on the floor, which left the bed, and that didn't seem appropriate. But that meant I had to somehow make it to the hallway in this getup.

"How's it going?" Jackson asked through the door.

I glanced down. The costume fit. That was a start. But I definitely needed to do some crunches before my abs would look good in this.

All in all, I was feeling self-conscious.

"Joey?"

"Don't make fun of me," I called, my fingers digging into the comforter beneath me.

"Of course I'm not going to make fun of you."

He was right. Jackson wasn't the type to make fun of me because of body image. He might tease me at times, but he was never mean.

Drawing in a deep breath, I stood and hopped to the door, wishing now that I'd never volunteered for this assignment. But there were no takebacks, not when I considered all the hoops that had been jumped through to get here.

Cora. Remember Cora. And Lexi.

I released my hair from the elastic holding it back and made sure it cascaded over my shoulders. The long locks made me feel more covered, more mermaidish. I shoved a strand behind my ear, drew in a deep breath, and then opened the door, ready to face my nemesis.

Jackson's eyes widened when he saw me. He looked me up and down and nodded slowly. "It . . . fits."

I nodded, unsure what I'd expected him to say. But of course he was keeping this professional. "It will take some getting used to. I'll wear it around my place tonight so I don't look awkward tomorrow."

"Whatever works for you." He stepped closer. "Lift your hair up for me."

My heart stammered in my ears, but I did as he asked. He scooted around me, resting his hand on my shoulder. Fire exploded in me at his touch as he inspected the back of the costume.

I felt all too aware of his every movement. Did he feel this tension also? Or was it just me?

"There's nowhere for a wire." He frowned and stepped back.

I bit back disappointment. He was all business. Of course. What did I think he was going to do? Make a comment about how good I looked dressed as a fish lady?

"But you'll be with me, right?" I said. "No need for a wire."

"We can use a parabolic mic. The officers hiding in the woods will be able to hear everything that way. Plus I'll have a wire."

"Sounds like all of our places are covered. I mean, bases. Our bases are covered. Not places . . . like bellies or anything."

His eyes finally met mine. "Sounds like it."

I pointed behind me, all too aware of Jackson's every move still. I was acting ridiculous! "I should go change then."

"As long as you think this costume will work."

"Of course. I've just got to learn how to

move—" As I said the words, I tried to hop forward. But the tail caught behind me, and I lost my balance. I began toppling backward.

I gasped, knowing without a doubt that this wasn't going to be pretty.

Before I hit the floor, Jackson's arms encircled me, sending even more heat through every part of me. He scooped me up, and my arms instinctively went to his neck.

Time seemed to slow. We stared at each other. My heart raced as if I'd just run a marathon.

Finally, Jackson cleared his throat and set me back on my feet. Er . . . fin? "You okay?"

I nodded, my cheeks on fire and my hands trembling. "Oh yeah, I'm fine. Great. Just have to get used to this . . . this outfit. Of course. It's got me off balance."

"Can you make it to the bed okay?"

More heat rushed to my cheeks, though I knew it was an innocent question. "Definitely."

No way was I letting him carry me there. I already looked like a bumbling fool as it was.

I grabbed the dresser, determined to save face. "I'll get changed and be right out."

Before he could say anything, I closed the door. So hard that it threw me off balance.

And I fell. Onto the floor. My elbows hit the

wood, and a moan escaped before I could stop it.

But at least the door was closed.

"Are you okay?" Jackson yelled.

"Just fine!" I called, already feeling an ache in my bones.

And then I promptly buried my head under my arms, wondering how I'd ever managed to play a character on TV who was so skilled and graceful.

CHAPTER 7

"I can't believe the police actually went for it," Zane said at my place that evening. *Splash* played in the background—the scene where Daryl Hannah comes ashore at the Statue of Liberty. You know . . . research. One never knew when a mermaid might have only six fun-filled days to be human while the moon was full.

"I know. I can't believe it either." I tried to squeeze past him but teetered. As I did, Zane pulled me down onto his lap.

"You're the prettiest mermaid I've ever seen." Zane's stare made his approval clear.

Even though I had pulled on a sweatshirt over the bikini top, just to make things feel a little more appropriate, I still felt exposed and silly.

"I feel like an idiot." I pulled my fin up beside me, and the silicon squealed in an embarrassing *whoosh* of air.

Zane was hanging out with me. Sometimes we met on our adjoining balconies at the end of the day, and sometimes we met outside. Either way, it usually ended with one or the other of us at one or the other's place. It was our little routine, and he seemed perfectly content to let me do what I needed to do while he chilled.

"I think we should reenact a scene from *The Little Mermaid*," Zane said. "Maybe they'll do a live action version of it, like they did with *Beauty and the Beast*, and you can be Ariel."

"That sounds like a filming nightmare. Especially for me, the queen of bloopers." I had to stop myself before I started to picture it too much.

I stared at the hummus and pita chips Zane held, really wanting one. But the other part of me didn't want to eat anything until after my photo op tomorrow. I'd been programmed by Hollywood to think this way. I supposed I'd had a choice in the matter, but undoing stinkin' thinkin' was hard.

I'd been judged for every visible inch of my body. My cellulite had been circled, highlighted, and expanded nearly to real-life size. It had been published, and people in grocery stores across the country could see it and revel in my lumpy fat.

One didn't get over that quickly.

It also didn't help that Eric had told me on

more than one occasion that I was hideous. That makeup artists did wonders with me. That if people could see how I really looked, I'd be laughed at and no one would put me on their "most beautiful" list.

As a hollow feeling formed in my gut, I pushed those thoughts aside. It would do no good to dwell on them.

Since I'd left the police station, I'd spent a considerable amount of time studying various poses I should use tomorrow. I was doing my research, just like any good actress preparing for a role. I really wished Yanic was here to help. But he was a long way from the OBX.

But I was getting nervous also. What if I couldn't pull this off? What if I tipped the photographer off? What if he did kill Cora? Would he try to kill me also?

I reviewed what I'd learned in my research. Apparently, professional mermaids were hired by aquariums, resorts, movie directors, event planners, corporate companies, fashion designers, and VIP parties. Also, each had her own *mer*sonality, as they called it. Some were seductive. Others perky. Still others were hippie inspired.

Most of them had to be avid swimmers, skilled at free diving. And they could hold their breath five minutes underwater. Five minutes? That was insane.

One lady had even developed a mermaid empire. Not only did she perform, but she had employees who were also professionals. They'd been all over magazines and TV. Sometimes they even performed for eight to twelve hours in tanks.

"What can I do?" Zane asked.

"Well, did you know that professional mermaids actually have people that they pay to cart them around? Some of them use an actual cart, and others use wheelchairs. All because it's so hard to walk in these things."

"I hereby volunteer to cart you around," he said.

"Do you?"

"But I won't be needing a cart." He stood with me in his arms. "I prefer to do it the old-fashioned way."

He twirled me around until my stomach rose and flopped like I was on a roller coaster. And I giggled.

My cell phone started playing "Under the Sea" just then. Yes, I'd programmed the tune to help me get into character. Zane set me down, and I glanced at the screen.

It was my bestie, Starla. I hadn't talked to her

in a few weeks because she was shooting a new movie on an island somewhere in the Pacific.

"Hey, Joey! How are things in Mule's Bottom?"

I hopped toward the corner for privacy and let out a small sigh. Starla and I had been over this before. "Nags Head."

"I can never get that right! It's such a peculiar name."

"Land pirates would tie lanterns around horse's necks and walk them up and down the dunes. It gave sea captains the impression that other boats were bobbing on the water. But they weren't, and the boats would crash on the shoals, and then these land pirates would grab their loot—" I stopped myself. I found all of this very fascinating, but not everyone did. "Anyway, how's Hollywood treating you?"

"I just finished shooting that romantic comedy. It was so fun, and Ryan Fowler is so cute, not the egomaniac I assumed he'd be. I've got a couple weeks off, and then I start shooting an indie film."

"An indie film?"

"Well, I figured *Island Fever* was a good business move, but this indie movie is a good heart move, you know? It won't be as mainstream, but I think it will make people stop pigeonholing me as eye candy and start thinking of me as a serious actress."

"That's important." The corner didn't quite offer the privacy I wanted, so I hopped out onto my balcony and looked at the stars sparkling overhead. Starla was beautiful and pretty superficial in a *Legally Blonde* kind of way, so I doubted people would ever take her too seriously. But I had to give her props for trying.

Her tone changed from cheerful to serious faster than a squall blowing in over the Atlantic. "Listen, did you hear that Eric is engaged?"

My throat tightened. I didn't even care about Eric anymore. But it was still weird hearing her announcement. "No, I hadn't heard. Tiffany, huh?"

"Yeah, I just found out. I wanted to make sure you heard from me before it showed up in the tabloids. It always shows up in the tabloids."

Eric had cheated on me with Tiffany. I was pretty sure he'd cheated on Tiffany with a girl he'd met while doing a guest role on *Grey's Anatomy*, where he'd played a patient struggling with impotence. I'd tried to tell Tiffany about his cheating ways once and had been accused of being jealous and wanting Eric for myself. Nothing could be further from the truth.

"Well, good for him," I finally said, closing my

eyes and listening to the waves. "I hope Tiffany is happier and safer with him than I was."

"We've all tried to warn her," Starla whispered. "Anyway, I heard another rumor, Joey. I hate to be the bearer of bad news. I'd much rather talk about Mule's Bottom or *Island Fever*."

I braced myself, not liking the ominous ring of her words. "Okay . . . Is it about the book Eric is supposedly writing about our relationship?"

I couldn't wait for that to hit the shelves. Sarcasm, just in case you were wondering. I'd talked to a lawyer who said he couldn't do anything. Go figure.

"No, I haven't heard anything else about that. But I was talking to Fred, who's friends with Arnold, who helps with the video editing for Alastair Productions. Anyway, long story short, you know that scene that was cut from *Family Secrets*?"

My mind raced through the possibilities. "I'm sure a lot of scenes were cut."

"I'm talking about the scene with Eric." Her words hung in the still, nighttime air.

The icky feeling in my gut grew even ickier. Eric had done a guest spot in the movie, playing a deliveryman who was secretly supplying a message to me from the Russian government. It was all cute when we were married. But I'd understood that scene had been cut.

"Yeah, they put that scene back in," Starla told me.

A surge of anger rushed through me. "Why would they do that?"

"For ratings, of course. Everyone knows how contentious your split was. They're doing to you what they did to Jennifer Aniston and Brad Pitt. They're capitalizing on your loss. I'm sorry, Joey. I wanted to be the first to tell you."

I was definitely going to be talking to Rutherford, my manager.

We chatted a few more minutes before I ended the call. As soon as I hopped back inside, Zane glanced at me.

"Everything okay?" Zane asked.

"No, not really." I plopped down beside him and wrapped myself in my grandmother's quilt. I'd found it in a trunk my father left behind, and since then, I'd wanted to cuddle with it every night. It somehow made me feel connected with my past, which was therapeutic because I felt desperately disconnected in general.

"What's wrong? Is it something a shoulder rub would help?"

"Unfortunately, no," I said. "I've got to go to a movie premiere."

And I'd see Eric. I never wanted to see Eric again, which was one more reason it was nice being here in North Carolina, miles and miles away from him.

"A movie premiere?" Zane's eyes lit. "It sounds fun."

"It's not that fun." There would be a lot of pictures on the red carpet. And I'd be there alone. Which would cause even more speculation and rumors. Meanwhile, Eric would be there with his new fiancée and look like the epitome of happiness.

"If you need someone to go and have your back, let me know," Zane said.

I smiled. "Thanks. I appreciate that."

"By the way, my GMRO video went viral— minus the mermaid tail portion, of course."

"Did it?" That wasn't really surprising. Zane knew his way around social media.

"That's, in part, thanks to you. Slick Ocean is thrilled."

"I'm glad I could help."

He rubbed his hands together, as if preparing for another adventure. "I've got to plan our next undertaking."

"It will have to be after my movie premiere."

He raised his eyebrows. "Or will it?"

I didn't know what that meant. But I didn't

have time to worry about it now.

***

"Are you sure you want to do this?" Jackson asked the next day. "It's not too late to change your mind."

"Yeah, I'll be totally fine." But I didn't feel totally fine. No, I'd considered changing my mind. Feigning some life or death hair emergency at Beach Combers. Maybe a last minute radio interview that I couldn't get out of contractually.

And then I'd remembered all those people I knew of who'd been taken advantage of in their quest for fame. I felt like I had to do this to help all of them. Moreover, there was an elaborate setup in place, and I couldn't let the department down.

"Besides, what can go wrong?" I said.

Jackson didn't say anything, and I knew what that meant. *Everything* could go wrong.

Sure, there would be officers set up in the woods. But things could spiral out of control. There were a lot of variables here.

But I didn't want to show my fear, so I put on my best actress face. "I'm ready."

I glanced up at my temporary "boyfriend." Jackson had been surprisingly transformed into the role. He wore baggy jeans, an old sweatshirt, and a baseball cap with aviator glasses.

He looked good. Then again, he looked good however he dressed.

"Let's do this," I announced. I hoped he couldn't see my nerves, because they'd captured me like opening night of a big play. Like *Romeo and Juliet*, if I had to choose. Except they'd both died at the end.

Lexi, I remembered. I was doing this for her. For justice. To let people who took advantage of others know they couldn't get away with it.

Jackson led me to a car the police department had loaned us and helped me into the passenger seat before climbing in himself. I tangled my fingers together in my lap as we started down the road. Octopus fingers, as Eric had called them.

"So the police aren't going to simply arrest this guy as soon as he shows up," I said, rehashing what I already knew.

"No, get him talking. We need to know this is the right guy first," Jackson said. "You remember the script we went over?"

"Of course."

"Any time you want out, just say that you're not feeling well. I'll get you out of there."

"Got it." No sooner had I said the words did

we pull up at the small parking lot near the public sound-access point.

I wore the mermaid top and boy-short bottoms beneath a sweatshirt and seashell leggings. Once I got on the shoreline, I'd tug on the mermaid tail. I'd taken special care to curl my hair in more of a mermaid style and to do my makeup, careful to add a little glitter on my face just for effect. I'd even found a mermaid necklace at one of the souvenir shops this morning and had donned that as well.

For right now, I wasn't Joey Darling or Raven Remington. I was Ari White, an overeager, giddy southerner living across the water in Hyde County. I wanted to enter a modeling contest and needed some new shots.

"Okay, let's do this." I extended my hand. "Boyfriend."

Jackson only hesitated a split second before grabbing my hand. We were now in full acting mode. I threw my bag with my mermaid tail over my shoulder, double-checked that I had my cash in my purse—five hundred dollars, as requested—and we walked onto the sand.

I liked holding Jackson's hand a little too much. It was strong, rough, and thick. It made my heart slow and my shakes cease slightly.

"Lo and behold, I think the photographer is

already here," I mumbled, nodding toward the man in the distance.

That had to be a good sign, right? If this man was guilty, would he really show up? Wouldn't he be hiding right now?

I quickly observed him. He was a fairly tall guy who I guessed was in his early thirties. His dark hair was slicked back from his face, his white shirt unbuttoned a little too much, and he wore multiple gold necklaces. All together I got a Fabio vibe from him.

He definitely looked big enough to take someone by force, if necessary. Was he the guy from the gas station? I didn't think so.

I was glad Jackson was with me.

I paused in front of Andre. But his gaze only remained on me a moment before fluttering to Jackson and darkening.

"Andre?" I started, using my best Valley girl voice. "I'm Ari."

He sauntered over, held me at arm's length, and gave me a once-over. "Beautiful. Just beautiful, *ma cherie*."

He kissed his hand and then exploded his fingers in the air. His French accent made me cringe. That couldn't be real. It just couldn't be.

But his gaze darkened again when he looked at Jackson. "And who's this *garcon*?"

"And this is my boyfriend, Sheldon. But I like to call him Shel. I think it's a nice name. Like Shel Silverstein. You know, the guy who wrote *The Giving Tree*. He doesn't think it's very masculine though." I let out a purposefully thin giggle and rested my hand on Jackson's chest. "I say he's a hubba hubba hunk, even if his nickname makes him sound like a conk. Isn't that right, Shel?"

Jackson smiled, looking surprisingly affable. "Whatever makes you happy."

Andre nodded, acting like he couldn't care less. "I see, even though I prefer to work alone. Boyfriends are . . ." He scowled at Jackson. "*La* distraction. I need you to promise me you'll be yourself. Be free. Embrace your inner siren."

Each word sounded guttural and was proceeded with a little spit.

"I'll send all those sailors to their death," I said.

Andre scrunched his eyebrows together in confusion.

"You know, in Greek mythology the sirens would sing and lead sailors to wreck their ships on the coasts," I explained. "They were originally not half-woman, half-fish at all, but half-woman, half-bird." I stopped and waved a hand in the air. "But we don't need a lesson on that, do we?"

Jackson snaked an arm around my waist.

"Beneath this bubbly facade is a straight-A student."

Andre smiled, though it looked forced. "Even better. *Jolie* and smart. My contacts in New York are going to *amour* you."

"I got a full ride at Yale, but all I want is to be a mermaid." I was improvising. Which could be good or bad. I had been an honor roll student, however. Book smart with no common sense. That was what my guidance counselor had told me once.

"You brought your mermaid costume, *oui*?"

I nodded. "Of *course*. It's like my second skin. I think I was a mermaid in a past life. Do you believe in mermaids, Andre?"

"I like mermaids. I think the idea is fascinating."

"Well, I think your pictures are fascinating. I love what you can do with the light." I'd looked at his fake website.

"I always say anyone can take a picture, but it takes a professional to know how to work the lighting." He kissed his fingers and waved them in the air with flourish again.

"I'd agree. Wouldn't you, honey?" I rested a hand on Jackson's chest and batted my eyelashes.

Jackson touched the tip of my nose. "Whatever you say, sweetie."

"Okay, what do you want me to do?" I looked around, knowing I had to break eye contact with Jackson before my pupils did that telltale dilating thing. "I think this is the perfect location."

"I like it here. It's *très magnifique*. It's easy to get to the water, and a lot of people don't know about it, so it's fairly private. I understand you want some shots for a portfolio? You'd like to do some modeling?"

I nodded. "It's my dream."

He squinted. "You look a *oui* bit familiar."

I wondered if he was trying to use the French word "*oui*" or "wee." "Oh, I get that all the time. I guess there's some actress that I resemble."

He shrugged, seeming to buy the excuse. "Okay then. Let's get started. You want to go ahead and get into costume?"

"Do I ever."

Feeling the slightest touch of self-consciousness, I kicked my flip-flops off, pulled off my leggings, and lowered myself onto a towel on the sand. I pulled my mermaid tail from my bag and shimmied into it.

My throat clamped with another rush of nerves as I took off my sweatshirt. I'd been like this on set also. The good girl who still valued modesty. My colleagues had made fun of me all the time.

Andre's eyes warmed with approval, but he tried to look away before I could see it.

"All right. Why don't you take your place by the water? I think it's going to be a *splendide* day to get some pictures."

I nodded, and Jackson took my arm to help me to the shoreline.

Andre arranged my fins in the water, where gentle waves lapped them. Then he arranged my hair and arms, down to the last detail. Jackson stood in the background with his arms crossed, watching everything and trying to appear like an overprotective boyfriend. I was pretty sure his gaze never left me.

"So you have connections in New York?" I asked, giving the camera my best runway stare.

Andre peered into his camera. "That is right. I worked there for eight years. Now I help models make the connections they need. I think you've got what it takes. Those cheekbones are *magnifiques*."

"That's great. All I've ever wanted to do is to be a mermaid and book gigs like this. Instead of paying, I want to get paid though." I raised my shoulder and peered over it, trying to look sassy but feeling ridiculous in the process.

He snapped another photo. "Well, I think you are on your way. You are *une naturelle*. And you've got great abs."

I sucked in again, not feeling at all like I had great abs. "Thanks. It's amazing what some lemon juice and cayenne pepper can do."

"Now let's get some with you on your stomach. Lift your feet up so we can see the fin."

I did as he directed.

"So do you do this a lot?" I asked.

He shrugged and snapped another picture. "I get around."

"Mostly here in the OBX?" I continued, trying to get more information out of him. "I have to admit that I'm kind of fascinated by you and your work." I glanced at Jackson. "No offense, Shelly Belly."

Jackson's eyes narrowed, but only for a split second. Then he smiled, looking lovelorn again.

"Up and down the coast, really." Andre continued working, which seemed like a convenient excuse for avoiding eye contact.

"But admit it: the Outer Banks is the best location ever."

That got a smile out of him. "It is a great place for pictures."

"I'm so curious about your career. Do you scout out models?"

He shrugged again. "Kind of. I'm very selective about whom I choose."

There it was. I heard it! It was a break in his accent. This man was not French. That fueled some kind of internal flame in me.

"What's the market like for mermaids?" I continued, pausing with my hand raked halfway through my hair.

"It is good. The market is pretty small, which actually opens up more opportunities for people who are good. People like you, *ma cherie*."

"I see. That's very exciting."

"I don't do very many shoots like this, but when I saw your photo, I knew I could not pass up this opportunity."

This was my opening! "It's funny because someone told me they saw another girl in a mermaid costume over at the preserve in Nags Head just a couple of days ago," I said. "She was having her pictures taken also."

"Is that right?" he asked, stiffening slightly.

I nodded. "And the strange thing is, she hasn't been seen since then."

"I see."

"I heard you might have been her photographer," I continued.

Fear flashed on the man's face. In the next instant, he took off in a run.

CHAPTER 8

Just as Andre tried to pass me, I swung my legs out. My mermaid tail tripped him, and he tumbled into the water. With his camera.

Even if he was a criminal, it kind of hurt to see the expensive equipment get ruined like that. Technology and the beach weren't good bedfellows.

Jackson jerked Andre to his feet as other officers emerged from the shrubs and dune grass around us. Andre would not be getting away now.

"You need to start talking," Jackson growled.

The man raised his hands, all signs of cockiness—and Frenchness—gone. He took a step back and looked over his shoulder. His head snapped forward. He'd probably realized he was surrounded.

"I didn't do nothing," he said.

His accent disappeared right along with his fake persona. Not only was he not French, but he also had a deep southern drawl. Fascinating.

"If you didn't do anything, why are you running?" Jackson growled, flashing his badge.

"Because something feels fishy here. Something besides a wannabe mermaid."

"I have no desire to be a mermaid, thank you very much." I leaned closer. "And I sold my role as the White Mermaid. I *sold* it."

Why did he have to bring a personal insult into this? Some people.

"Where's Cora Day?" Jackson demanded.

"Who?"

"Don't play dumb." Jackson leered at him. "You took pictures of her two days ago, and now she's gone."

He raised his hands higher. "I promise. I didn't do nothing. She was alive and kicking when I left her after our photo shoot."

Jackson bristled. "So you admit that you took pictures of her?"

"Yes, I did. Okay. I admit that." His words came out faster and faster. "But I didn't hurt her. Why would I do that?"

"You tell me."

"I'm innocent!"

"Then start talking before I take you down to the station," Jackson growled.

"Look, Cora wanted me to take some photos of her. So I did. I told her I'd have some images ready for her in two weeks, we said goodbye, and I went to my car. Job done."

"You left her at the beach, is what you're saying?" Jackson asked.

"Yes, that's exactly what I'm saying. She said she wanted to stay for a few minutes and enjoy the beauty around her. Her words, not mine."

"And nothing funny happened while you were there? Nothing that raised any red flags?"

"No, nothing. It was quiet. Peaceful. Beautiful."

I managed to get to my feet—no easy task, mind you—and made my way over toward them. I had some pressing questions of my own, despite my undocumented—I'd deny it if anyone asked—keep-my-mouth-shut clause.

"Why Nags Head Woods?" I asked.

"Because that's the location she requested. She said she'd always wanted to see that area."

"You really don't have any connections with New York," I muttered. He was running a scam. A very expensive scam. No doubt, he made promises he knew he couldn't keep.

He cringed. "Okay, not really."

"You're a con artist who preys on other people's desire to make it big. That's despicable. And vile. And you should be in jail."

"Read my contract. I've done nothing wrong. I

do send the shots to people in New York."

"Just like they could do themselves. You're not a talent scout, and you have no personal connections. That's just wrong." I leaned closer. "Did you even take those pictures on your website?"

I'd checked his website, and his pictures had been top grain. Suspiciously top grain.

When he said nothing, I knew the truth. No, he hadn't. He probably stole them from some stock-photo sites, if I had to guess.

"What about an umbrella?" I continued. "Did Cora use one for her photo shoot?"

His face wrinkled in off-putting confusion. "An umbrella? Like a beach umbrella? No, why would she do that? Mermaids don't use beach umbrellas."

I shrugged. "Just curious."

"We're going to need to see those pictures of Cora," Jackson said.

"That's a problem."

"Why?"

"Because someone stole my camera."

"When did that happen?" Jackson asked.

"Right after the photo shoot. I left the camera in the car and ran in to pay for some gas. When I got back, my camera was gone."

"Where'd you get the one you used today

then?" Jackson asked.

"A pawn shop. I'm barely making ends meet. Without a camera, I can't do photo shoots, so I had little choice but to buy a new one. It was painful though."

"Mark, take him down to the station, and see if his story checks out." Jackson handed him off to another officer. "I'll be there in a few minutes."

Andre was still talking, yammering away, as Mark and two other officers led him to a patrol car. When they were out of sight, I turned to Jackson, feeling a touch of triumph.

"I totally know what my tweet blitz is going to be for this. First day with the Hashtag: NHPDBlue is a success. Just call me Dennis Franz, only prettier." I made duck lips and posed like a hip-hop star. "And even better, I didn't ruin things!"

I reached forward to give Jackson a high five. As I did so, I lost my balance and face-planted in the sand.

***

When everyone had left, Jackson turned to me there on the sandy shores. I pulled my sweatshirt closer, and my stomach grumbled, reminding me how hungry I was. The good news was that I no longer wore the mermaid tail and now donned some comfy leggings instead.

"How'd you know about the umbrella stand?" Jackson's laser-beam gaze sliced into me.

My cheeks heated. I'd been caught! Again! *Daggonit!* Jackson wasn't supposed to know that I knew about that. "Didn't you mention it?"

"No, I didn't." He turned away from the sun glaring behind me. "Joey, have you been investigating again? On your own?"

"Investigating would be a strong word. I was just asking some questions."

He let out a sigh. "Joey, have you not learned anything from the last two investigations you got tangled up in?"

"What do you mean? I helped solve them, didn't I? Maria Salvatore would agree, as would millions of her viewers."

"And you almost got yourself killed in the process."

"Almost is the key word here." If in doubt, keep it light. It'd always worked for me in the past.

"I'm serious, Joey." And for Jackson, if in doubt, keep everything heavy enough to sink like an anchor.

I had no question about the fact he was serious. I pushed my hair away from my face, buying myself a moment of thought. "Is that the only reason you agreed to bring me along with you? You want to keep an eye on me and keep me out of trouble."

"Someone has to!"

I raised my chin and crossed my arms in defiance. I didn't want to be a thorn in his side, yet I was certain he viewed me that way. Nor did I want him to feel like he had to babysit me. No thank you.

"I never asked anyone to be my guardian. I'm doing just fine on my own." I was actually doing terrible on my own, but I wouldn't admit it right now.

"No one does just fine on their own, Joey. Life isn't designed to work like that."

"Sometimes a person doesn't have any choice." I hadn't intended to admit that. To have this argument. To face off against Jackson.

Neither of us spoke. We stared at each other, tension stretching between us.

Until his phone rang. He mumbled a few things into it before turning to me.

"There's someone at the station who claims to have some answers," he said. "Let's go."

***

Jackson and I hardly said anything to each other on the drive back to police headquarters. I had so many thoughts running through my head, starting with: How could I have been so stupid to mention that umbrella stand? That quickly morphed into, why couldn't Jackson just appreciate me for doing a good job out there? I'd totally nailed it as the White Mermaid.

Before we walked inside the police station, Jackson turned to me in all of my wannabe mermaid glory. "I'm meeting with one of Cora's friends, Rachel Lewis. You can listen in as I talk to her. But that's it." He sliced his hand through the air. "You're simply there to observe. If you step out of line, I'll have to ask you to leave."

Offense rose in me. Jackson had no faith in me. No faith at all. And I didn't appreciate it.

Yet I didn't want to miss this opportunity. "Fine."

I wanted to change into some jeans and a nice shirt, but instead I'd leave on my leggings and sweatshirt. It didn't look professional, but at least I wasn't still wearing a mermaid tail. From what I gathered by eavesdropping on Jackson's phone conversation on the way here, another detective was going to interrogate Andre. I had a feeling the man wasn't guilty. That was simply based on a gut feeling that had formed while watching his reactions to our questions. I felt pretty confident that Jackson was on the same page.

We walked into his office, and a woman sat in a chair there. Officer Loose Lips—also known as Danny Something or Other—stood beside her, waiting for Jackson to arrive.

I'd given several of the officers here nicknames. Officer Always Serious Byron. Officer I Like Duck Donuts Windsor. Officer Thick Neck Jenkins.

Jackson gave Loose Lips a subtle nod, and the rookie officer departed like a well-trained lackey.

How did Jackson do that? Wherever he went, he seemed to command respect. But it was so subtle.

And so appealing.

Which was so stupid. Because the man drove me crazy. I didn't even *like* him half the time. Yet he was crazy attractive to me.

Which was just one more way I always got myself in trouble: men.

I glanced at the woman sitting in front of Jackson's desk. She was youngish. Maybe in her twenties, but she could easily pass for a teen. She had dirty-blond hair that fell below her shoulders, and pale skin with numerous blemishes—dark circles, a smattering of zits, poorly applied makeup. She wore tight jeans and a cheap T-shirt.

I kind of wanted to give her a day at the spa, complete with a facial and some highlights. Some people just couldn't catch a break, and I had a feeling Rachel was one of those people.

"Rachel." Jackson extended his hand. "I'm Detective Sullivan. This is Ms. Darling. She's just here to observe."

He emphasized the word *observe*. Loser.

Rachel's eyes widened when she saw me. I had that effect on people. Sometimes because I was famous, and other times because I was so oblivious.

"You're doing research, aren't you?" Rachel said, still staring. "Do you have a new show coming up? I can't wait to see *Family Secrets*. It looks like a blockbuster. You and Jessica Alba? How could you go wrong?"

"Thanks." I clearly felt the dirty look Jackson gave me.

He didn't seem to appreciate it when other people admired me. Did he not think acting was commendable? Maybe he simply resented my presence.

"If Cora knew you were helping search for her, she would just flip. She loved your show, and she heard you were in this area. She talked about coming down sometime just to see if she could spot you. Maybe even take a selfie together."

"I'm . . . flattered."

"She mourned for days when you and Eric split," Rachel continued, Jackson's presence seemingly long forgotten. "She thought you two were perfect together. She was all like, if they can't make, then what makes me think I can make it with Elrod?"

"Things aren't always what they appear on the surface." The words hurt as they left my lips. But I didn't want anyone to hold up Eric and me as the standard for a perfect relationship.

"At least you were able to hook up with that hot surfer. I saw it online somewhere."

"We haven't hooked up," I corrected. "I'm single. Totally single right now."

"For real?" She looked disappointed.

It was so hard living someone else's fantasy.

Okay, now I desperately wanted Jackson to take over this conversation. "For real. So, about Cora . . ."

"Right." Rachel straightened. "Cora. Any updates on her?"

Just then, another officer brought in three cups of coffee. Jackson took a seat behind the desk, and I stood against the wall, where any good *observer* might. I took a sip of the police department–grade coffee and nearly spit it out. It tasted like it should have grounds floating inside it. I looked more closely. It *did* have grounds floating in it.

"We were hoping you might have information for us that would help," Jackson said, wisely ignoring his cup of hot java. He could have warned me, at least. Double loser.

"No, I haven't heard from her since she left to come down here."

"Was she having any trouble with anyone?" Jackson asked.

"Besides her boyfriend?"

Jackson crossed his very able arms over his very defined chest. "Tell us about that."

"Well, Elrod might seem like a nice enough guy, but he was slightly controlling. He didn't want her to go do this photo shoot. At all." Rachel's hands flew through the air as she spoke.

"Why not?" Jackson asked.

"He was afraid that fame would change her. That he'd lose her. That's my theory at least." She glanced back at me. "You know all about that, huh, Joey?"

I drew in a shaky breath and forced a smile. That was how my father must have felt when I left for Hollywood. And he was right. "Fame is a beast that not many people can tame."

"Oh my goodness. That's a great quote. I love it."

"I try." I totally needed to tweet that. Hashtag: inspirationwhileonthesetofNHPDBlue.

"About Cora . . ." Jackson said, trying to keep us on track.

"The first chance Cora got, she was going to break away from this small town. She wanted to go to LA or New York."

"And become a professional mermaid?" I asked, still stunned that people took mermaid-dom so seriously.

"Well, that was one of her plans. She would have taken any modeling gig. Or maybe a role in a soap opera. She'd even applied for some game shows."

"Her end goal was fame, in other words," I muttered, leading to another scowl from Jackson. I was supposed to stay quiet.

"I guess you could say that. She kind of stumbled into the mermaid thing by accident. She was wearing her costume at the beach and then was asked to do a few parties in the area. Then she did a couple of gigs at the aquarium. People seemed to really like her. She thought that might be a good way to break in."

Jackson started to say something, but I had to jump in. Again.

"What do you mean parties? Like kid parties?" I just couldn't figure this out.

"No, like grown-men parties. Women too, I guess, though all Cora talked about was the men. It was kind of weird."

This sounded like the start of something ugly. Really ugly. "Where were these parties?"

"Here. In the Outer Banks. They were very posh, apparently. That's how Cora made it sound."

"What did she do while there?" I continued.

"She wore her mermaid costume. Mingled. Added atmosphere, I guess."

Jackson threw me a stern glance. "Did Elrod approve of these parties?"

Rachel shrugged. "Cora didn't tell him she was going."

Jackson's eyes narrowed, and he tapped his fingers together. "Do you think Elrod would hurt her?"

Rachel frowned and adjusted her legs in the seat, pulling them both toward her and looping her arms around her knees. "I'm not sure. I'd like to say no. That's my first instinct. But who really knows anyone?"

"One more question," Jackson said. "Why did she choose Nags Head Woods for her photo shoot? Do you know?"

She twisted her lips. "She seemed obsessed with the area lately."

"What do you mean?" Jackson asked.

"I don't know. I mean, she always liked it there, but even more so lately. This newfound obsession started a few days ago. I caught her doing some research online. Then she took me hiking there one day, but she didn't seem all chill, if you know what I mean. She kept looking around, like she was lost or something. And she refused to stay on the trails. She said it was more fun if we did our own thing." She froze. "I'm not going to get arrested for that or anything, am I?"

Jackson shook his head before narrowing his eyes in thought. "Did you ask her about it?"

"I was like, what's your problem? And she was like, nothing, why? I was like, because you're acting all weird. And she was like, no, I'm not. And I was like, you totally are."

Jackson raised a hand. "I get it. So you have no clue why she liked it so much?"

She shook her head. "No, not a single one."

***

Back at home, I had to talk to Zane. Because if anyone knew about parties in this area, it was Zane. He was a regular social butterfly with more friends than a migration of monarchs. Rachel's revelation about Cora working parties in the OBX seemed like the next possible lead as to where to look for answers.

As soon as Zane answered the door, I charged into his duplex, my mind racing a million miles a minute. I just hoped he didn't have any women there—either massage clients or new girlfriends I didn't know about.

Story of my life.

"What's going on?" He shut the door and followed behind me, munching on some peanuts.

I seriously wished I had his metabolism. I'd been so hungry on the way home from the police station that I'd gone through a drive-through. Of a fast-food restaurant. And I'd gotten a fatty hamburger loaded with mayonnaise and cheese, as well as some french fries. That I'd dipped in ranch dressing.

My stomach already felt three inches larger than it had been earlier.

"Who in this area might have parties with mermaids?" I blurted, forcing myself to focus.

Zane twisted his head in thought. "Besides people in their mer-kingdom and little children who love Disney cartoons?"

"I'm being for real. Yes. Not kids." I lowered my voice. "You know what I mean."

"Sorry, sorry. I was wrapped up in my Bob Ross Zen." He closed his eyes a moment. "Let me change gears."

I paced, knowing I probably wasn't making a lick of sense but charging forward anyway. "Apparently, there are people in this area who have parties and pay people dressed as mermaids to come entertain. Do you know who?"

I followed Zane as he walked into the kitchen and turned off a small TV in the corner where *The Joy of Painting* played. He took his place behind a cutting board and began to chop vegetables that were already laid out. Based on the juicer on the counter, he was going to make a tasty drink.

In between eating peanuts.

"Mermaid parties sound very lavish and colorful," he said, chopping some celery.

"You're still not answering my question." I stopped pacing for long enough to stare at him.

He continued chopping. "I'm guessing whoever is attending these parties may not be full-time residents but people from out of town."

"I thought this was a family vacation town?"

He shrugged. "It usually is. But there are always outliers."

"Have you ever been invited to a party like that? An outlier party?"

His cheeks reddened ever so slightly, but he continued chopping. "Maybe once."

"Who threw it?"

He fidgeted. Why didn't he want to tell me? There was more to this story; I was sure of it.

"Zane?" I waited, giving no indication of giving up this interrogation.

He let out a deep breath and paused from his moment of vegetable bliss. "Billy. Billy had a party like that a month or so ago. He's probably had more since then."

"Billy Corbina from Willie Wahoo's?" The man had always remained a sketchy character in my mind. His dad was one of the wealthiest men in the area. Though I had no confirmation that Billy was into anything illegal, I had my suspicions. I also wondered if he might know something about my father's disappearance.

Zane nodded. "Yep, the one and only."

"Did you go?"

He took a bite of a carrot. "No, I didn't go. He's usually up to trouble. He always has been."

I stopped in the middle of my mad pacing. "You mean, you've known Billy since he was younger?"

"We went to high school together."

I nodded slowly, letting that sink in. I knew Zane had done drugs back then, and now I wondered what kind of role Billy may have played in that. I'd bet there was a connection.

I pressed my hands on the counter. "What happens at those parties, Zane?"

He stepped back, and I could see the tension on his features. Not the best look for a person with a knife in his hands. "My best guess? Drugs. Women. Gambling. Who knows what else? Nothing I want to be a part of."

"Why would Billy have mermaids there?"

"I'm sure it just adds to his over-the-top effect."

"What is that?"

"You know, you see it on TV all the time. Those rich men who have fancy parties with scantily clad women. I'm sure that had something to do with it. I prefer not to know all the details. Billy tries to be flashy, to remain the big fish in a small pond. He's created almost a club-feel, invitation-only party."

I shoved my hip against the counter. "Zane, I need to go to one of those parties."

He started chopping again. "I can't help you there, Joey. I'm not going to put you in that position. No way."

Great. Now he was sounding like Jackson. If there was one thing I could always count on, it was that Zane wasn't like Jackson.

Except, now he was.

"Zane, someone at one of those parties might know where Cora is."

"So tell the police. Let them handle it."

"The people at those parties aren't going to tell the police anything. You and I both know it."

He finally put down his knife and pressed his palms into the counter as he stared at me, full attention engaged. "And how are you planning on finding out? They'll tell a celebrity instead?"

"I haven't thought it through. Maybe."

He remained stoic a minute before shaking his head again. "I can't do it."

My stubbornness kicked into gear like a race car headed toward the finish line in the Indy 500. "Fine. I'll find a way to do it myself then."

No man was an island.

It was a good thing I was a woman.

CHAPTER 9

Trying to find Cora made me feel fulfilled, like I was doing something useful. There was a lot to be said for that. I couldn't make it up to Lexi Pennington, but maybe I could make a difference to Cora. I knew that with every minute that passed, the likelihood of finding her diminished . . . just like with my dad.

That was why I went to Willie Wahoo's. It wasn't my favorite place, even though they did have a decent vegan menu. The bar and grill was trouble. Jackson had told me that before. Bar fights and all kinds of other illegal activities occurred there.

Despite that, I parked and strode inside, making a beeline for the bar. That was where Billy, also known as Mr. Clean because of his resemblance to the character of the same name, was standing, talking to someone and drying a glass.

He did a double take when he saw me.

He was like a tiger watching in the distance. He'd never done anything to directly put me on guard, but I couldn't help but think he looked at me as if I were prey.

"If it isn't Joey Darling. What brings you in here? You going to blow everyone away with some karaoke again? Maybe do a number from *Saturday Night Fever* this time?"

Billy had wrangled Zane and me—well, Zane hadn't needed to be convinced—to sing karaoke before he'd give us answers about a former case.

I shook my head and leaned against the bar, trying to look all casual-like. "I have a proposal for you."

"Is it an indecent one?"

"You're indecent." *Great comeback, Joey. If you're a ten-year-old.*

He raised his eyebrows and continued to dry glasses. "Okay."

"So I'm trying to make some money between my acting gigs. Back in LA I used to do some endorsement deals with local clubs and hot spots. I hear you're the person to talk to about doing that in this area."

"Did you?" His voice remained even and steady, not giving a clue to what he was thinking.

"I want to go to one of your parties."

"And do what?"

I shrugged, tapping into my acting skills now. This wasn't me. I didn't want to be a party girl. I'd made mistakes in the past, but I was a good girl. "I want to make a paid appearance."

He smirked. "What kind of parties do you think I have?"

"The fun kind." *Lame, Joey. Lame.*

He let out a chuckle. "Yeah, they're fun."

"Listen, I'm not talking anything inappropriate—or indecent. I just thought it could be fun if I made an appearance and gave some autographs."

"Because that's what we do at my parties? Stalk celebrities?"

I put a hand on my hip. "What do you do, Billy? Why don't you tell me?"

He leaned closer and lowered his voice. "Things that could make you blush."

To my dismay, I blushed. "Okay then. Offer rescinded. Thanks for the talk."

I started to walk away, when Billy called me back.

"Wait, Joey."

I paused, unsure what I hoped for. A change of mind? The opportunity to walk away before I got in trouble? The relief of being able to claim I'd tried, but it hadn't worked out?

"I might have something for you," he started.

"Maybe for the first part of the party anyway. You know, maybe you could make an appearance. I could slip you some money for showing up. We'll need a contract."

I raised my chin, remembering my cover was that I needed money. "How much money?"

"A couple grand. How's that sound?"

"It sounds mighty cheap, but since you're a new kid on the block in this department, I suppose it will do. It might make some of my debt collectors happy. When's the party?"

"Tomorrow. Are you available?"

"I'll make myself available."

"Great. Give me your number. I'll text you the details. Oh, and we have a confidentiality clause. You leak word of this to anyone, and there will be confidential consequences that you don't want to face."

I swallowed hard. I didn't like the sound of that. Not one bit.

But it was too late to back out now.

***

I was antsier than a bear in a beehive the next morning.

I couldn't pull this off.

I shouldn't even try.

To make it worse, business was slow at Beach Combers. Zane was working. Jackson was working. Or maybe not talking to me. I wasn't sure.

Phoebe wasn't at work at Oh Buoy. Rutherford wasn't answering the phone even.

So I did the only thing I could think of. I slipped into the back of Beach Combers and jumped on the computer to do research.

After I did that research, I composed some new tweets and sent them to the police chief for approval.

I checked the upcoming buzz for *Family Secrets*.

I looked at Zane's blog post on the Goat Man. One million hits and counting.

I clicked Play and watched the video a minute. I had to admit, it was good. He'd done a great job editing it to look like *The Blair Witch Project*. And the two of us looked like we were having a great time together.

That was because we were. We always had a good time together.

Unless he pretended to be Jackson. And then all the warm fuzzies quickly went away.

I had room for only one Jackson in my life.

At the last minute, I typed Lexi Pennington into the search engine. Lexi's picture filled the page, and my heart sagged.

Lexi had been nineteen when she died. She'd been pretty enough to make it big with her bright-blue eyes, auburn hair, and wide smile. But she'd been desperate. That desperation had led her to do unwise things.

She'd been so hopeful that day she'd cornered me at the coffee shop. She'd gushed about how much she admired me. She'd begged me to help her.

I'd been with Eric. He'd been impatient and ready to leave.

I'd tried to encourage her, to let her know it wasn't easy to catch a break. She'd asked for my number, but I hadn't given it to her. And then Eric had pulled me away.

Later, Lexi had tried to contact me through Facebook. The truth had been that I had only so many hours in my days, and I'd felt stretched so thin. I was approached for advice like that often. It wasn't humanly possible to respond to it all.

But if I had responded, how might things be different? Would Lexi be alive?

Guilt pounded at me.

I sighed and closed the computer. All of this was only accomplishing one thing: it was distracting me from the task at hand.

Tonight I was going to swim with sharks. And

I hoped to come out alive in the end.

CHAPTER 10

So I was nervous—more nervous than I thought I would be—before heading to one of Billy's wild parties.

What exactly would I be walking into?

Even worse, I didn't have Zane or Jackson at my side, watching my back. I usually had at least one of them with me, either adventurously willingly or begrudgingly out of obligation.

But Zane had been busy all day today showing a client some houses for sale in the area, all the way from Corolla at the northern end of the Outer Banks, down to Hatteras at the southern end. And Jackson . . . well, of course I couldn't tell him what I was doing. He would have probably handcuffed me to my oven door in order to keep me away.

Maybe it was better this way. At least no one could try to stop me. I knew this had bad idea written all over it, but I had to do it. It was my chance to figure out if these parties had something to do with Cora's disappearance. I needed to hook the bad guy and reel him in.

As promised, Billy had texted me the details of the soiree. I had to be at a huge oceanfront home at nine. And I had to wear a little black dress. My role would be to make people feel welcome.

Whatever that meant.

I pinched the skin between my eyes as I drove down Beach Road. Did I even want to find out? I wasn't sure. But I wasn't backing out now.

As always, I checked out a few episodes of *Relentless* before I left home. Raven always had some good tips to apply to these kinds of situations. *Keep the upper hand. Don't get cornered. Never turn your back on a crowd.*

I shoved down my nerves as I pulled into the driveway. There were already probably ten other cars at the house. Nice cars. Foreign cars. *Luxury* cars. Almost every window blazed with light, and I could hear music before I even opened my door.

I'd always hated these kinds of parties.

If my dad knew I was going to something like this . . . he would have a fit. He'd warned me against hanging out with people like this. *You become like the people you hang around. If you lie down with dogs, you'll wake up with fleas. Birds of a feather flock together.*

But I was going to do this anyway.

I walked toward the front door, pulling a gauzy shawl over my shoulders. It was too cold out here to wear just a little black dress with spaghetti straps. Besides, being instructed on how to dress made me feel like a piece of meat. Which was probably what Billy thought I was, because he was that kind of guy.

As soon as I knocked, a man I didn't know, who'd obviously been drinking too much, answered. Not only did he smell like alcohol, but he had a beer in his hand. His words slurred. And all his inhibitions seemed to be gone. Already.

The man had ruddy skin, orange-blond hair, and he wore too much gold jewelry. The look screamed, "I've got money. Pay attention to me!"

"Well, hello there." He wasn't looking at my eyes as a dopey grin splayed across his lips. "Come on in, beautiful."

I flashed a smile, wishing I felt at ease. But I didn't. "I guess I'm at the right place."

"I'd say you are." The jerk's eyes were still not on mine. "I'm Siegfried, by the way."

"Do you tame tigers?"

"Depends if you want to be a tiger." His eyes twinkled suggestively.

I needed to change the subject, and pronto. "I'm Joey."

He took my hand and kissed it, his lips wet and sloppy. "Pleasure to meet you, Joey."

I pulled away and drew my shawl closer as I stepped inside. "I'm here to see Billy."

"That's too bad," he muttered before yelling, "Billy! You've got someone here to see you!"

A moment later, Billy appeared at the door, also holding a bottle in his hands. He gave me a cold nod. "Joey. Come on in."

I followed after him.

Music assaulted my ears. Was this just a frat party for men who didn't want to outgrow their immaturity? Who wanted to feel like the Outer Banks had an elite club for the single and wealthy?

Only I had a feeling there was much more going on here right now than youthful fantasies. I just had to figure out what. Drugs? Quite possibly. Gambling? Another strong possibility.

As I walked through the house, I took note of everything around me, starting with how spacious this place was. It was beautiful and open and modern. A deejay played music in the background. Disco lights flashed. People danced.

Everyone I passed screamed wealth and affluence, from their clothes to the way they kept themselves. This was a different clientele than Willie Wahoo's. If I had to guess, these people valued their privacy and liked to be among people considered their equals. There were mostly men here, but I also spotted a few women. Two were dressed as mermaids, one as an Egyptian princess, and another as a scantily clad cowgirl.

I stored those facts away.

"Back here," Billy barked.

With a little more than a touch of hesitation, I followed him down a hallway and into a dimly lit bedroom. He picked up a paper and a pen and thrust them into my hands.

"What's this?" I asked.

"A contract saying you agree to stay for two hours, to mingle and act as a hostess, and that I'll pay you two thousand dollars, as per our agreement."

My stomach clenched. After I signed this, there was no backing out. But this was what I needed to do to find out answers.

I licked my lips, signed on the dotted line, and handed everything back to Billy. "Here you go."

"Now get out there and make me proud," Billy grumbled. "Don't make me regret this."

My limbs trembled ever so slightly as I stepped back into the hallway. A catchy tune by Rihanna blared, and I already felt a headache coming on.

I needed to get a better feel for this place before jumping into full acting mode. As I wandered through the living room, I noted that most of the party was outside. It was cold, but three outdoor heaters blasted warm air.

This whole thing felt slimy.

I should have never agreed to come here. What had I been thinking? But it was too late to leave now.

"Okay, your job is to mingle," Billy told me, coming up behind me, his breath hot on my ear. "Make everyone feel special."

I stared out at the crowd of mostly men.

"Define 'feel special.'" I didn't like the sound of that.

Billy smiled for the first time. "You'll figure it out. You do a good job, and I'll have that check waiting for you."

No way would I actually take cash for being here, no matter how much it could come in handy. If I did that, it might make me some kind of accessory to sleaziness. I was undercover. End of story.

I was an actress. I could do this.

I turned toward the crowd and unleashed the extrovert in me. "Who wants to have a good time?"

Several people cheered back.

"Then let's get this party started!"

***

So far I'd established that most of the people here were indeed wealthy and liked to talk about themselves. A lot. I'd met developers. Yacht builders. Restaurateurs. People who didn't seem to want to mix with the *hoi polloi*.

What I hadn't discovered was a motivation for someone to murder Cora.

I took a breather from dancing for long enough to grab some seltzer water from the bartender. Then I stood back, trying to form a game plan. Before I could, a man approached me.

"Aren't you Joey Darling?" He swirled the glass of hard liquor in his hand.

He was tall with dark-blond hair parted sharply on the side and heavily gelled. He wore a silky-looking black V-neck with a casual gray blazer. Something about the tautness of his face made me wonder if he'd had a facelift, even though I'd only guess him to be in his forties.

I nodded at his question. "The one and only."

"You've gone from being on TV to doing this?" He chuckled, and in that one little reaction, I recognized what he was doing: trying to put me in my place. Put me down. Make me feel small.

This man reminded me of Eric. Maybe it was his demeanor. Maybe the way he styled his hair with a harsh part and lots of gel. Maybe the way he put others down in order to make himself feel bigger and better.

I pushed aside my feelings. "Billy wanted to surprise everyone with an appearance by me. Don't worry—I'm being paid a pretty penny."

The man chuckled. "Now *that* sounds like Billy."

I settled against the wall, where I had a good view of everyone. Though the party had seemed to start on the deck, people had gravitated inside as a sharp wind stirred. The great room was crowded and loud, and the flashing lights were giving me a headache. Plus, it was hard to talk over the pulsating tunes of Chris Brown's club remix.

"I didn't catch your name," I said.

"Rupert."

"Do you know Billy well, Rupert?"

He shrugged, making it clear he had no loyalty to the party's host. "We hang in the same circles."

I raised my glass. "And what do you do in those circles?"

"Party. Why do you ask?" His voice decidedly changed from flirty to menacing.

"Researching a role. Of course." That was always my excuse. Research. And most of the time it worked. I really wanted to walk away from this conversation right now, but I couldn't. Guys like this were the kind who could give me clues about what happened to Cora. I had to stick this out for a little longer.

He nodded slowly. "Makes sense, I guess. The fast crowd in a slow town."

"Precisely. I'm trying to get a vibe on this kind of scene. It's so different from LA."

"It doesn't have to be different. What? Aren't we rich enough for you?" He raised his glass and took a sip.

"I don't know. I'm still trying to figure out how you're all rich and why you're all partying in secret like this."

His gaze darkened. "There's something about the girls Billy likes to bring here. They're too curious."

My pulse spiked before pounding with a dull throb in my ears. "What do you mean?"

He shrugged. "There was another girl here last time. She kept asking questions and acting peculiar. Asked about my car, my job, my jewelry even. Then she left early. Billy wasn't happy."

Cora. That had to be Cora.

"Maybe something spooked her." Maybe

someone spooked her. Someone like *you*.

"I was a perfect gentleman."

I doubted that. "Anyone here give her a hard time? I mean, why else would she leave early?"

"Good question. Don't know. Don't care." He flicked something invisible from his shirt.

I needed to change the subject before he got suspicious. I raised my glass of seltzer water, trying to look casual. "So you never said how you got rich."

"We have our ways around here."

"And what are those ways? Inspire me."

He shook his head and clucked his tongue. "That will cost you something."

Oh no, I wasn't about to find out what that meant. I needed to move on.

"It's been real," I said. Raven always said that, and it sounded so mysterious.

It seemed to work now also.

I wandered over to the next group, a set of equally unimpressive men doing much of the same thing as everyone else here. Drinking, talking, lurking.

Before I could initiate a conversation, Billy came over and draped his arm across my waist. "You guys met our guest of honor Joey Darling yet? She's so graciously agreed to help here. Just for a refresher, she was named as *People* magazine's fifty most beautiful stars last year. I'd say they got it right."

I actually blushed. It didn't matter how rich or famous I was. Deep inside, I was still the down-home girl from the mountains. I had no game. Not really.

"You brought in the big guns," one of the men said. "Impressive."

"I try." Billy's hand wandered a little too low, and I spun away from him.

"I need to keep mingling."

But I felt Billy's eyes on me as I walked away.

He was more of a snake than I'd thought he was.

I didn't realize until that moment just how tight my lungs felt. Really tight. Tight enough that I wanted to run from here. I wasn't part of this world, just like Ariel wasn't part of the world on the land.

But I couldn't leave. Not yet. Because I hadn't found out anything about Cora yet.

CHAPTER 11

Just as I started talking to another cluster of men, I saw one of the women dressed as a mermaid step outside. I excused myself from the conversation, seeing a clear opportunity to dialogue with her. When I slipped through the sliding glass doors, I spotted her near the pool with a cigarette in hand.

"Need a break?" I asked.

The woman's eyes widened, and she snubbed out her cigarette on the bar-height table beside us. "You're Joey Darling."

"I am. And who are you?"

"I'm Amy." Amy looked to be in her late teens. She had stick-straight, long black hair. Her thin body was accented with numerous tattoos, and she gave off somewhat of a Goth vibe.

"Nice to meet you. I needed a breather also, so when I saw you come out here, I wondered why I hadn't thought of this earlier."

"Yeah, there are too many hormones in there. Sometimes, I just need to get away."

"You sound like you've done this before." I gravitated toward the outdoor heater, already feeling chilled as the wind swept across the cool ocean. It had the same effect as a fan blowing over an ice cube.

She shrugged. "Third time."

"Is it a charm, like they say?"

She snorted. "That's not the way I'd word it."

"How did Billy find you?"

"We met at Willie's. He asked if I wanted to make some extra money."

I wondered if that was how Cora ended up here also.

"It feels weird being here," I said, glancing inside at the partygoers.

"It is. But there's nothing inappropriate. I guess the men feel more manly if there are pretty women around. And it helps to pay my bills, so why not? Mermaid for hire. That's me."

I leaned against the table, trying not to appear overly eager. "Did you meet someone here last week? A girl named Cora?"

She pulled out another cigarette. "Do you mind?"

I hated cigarettes, but I had a feeling smoking would put her at ease. "Go ahead."

She pulled a lighter from her bikini top and lit up. "Actually, I did meet Cora."

140

"Did you hear she disappeared?"

The girl's eyes widened. "No, I didn't. I don't keep up with the news too much. I'm too busy with college. What happened?"

"They don't know." I leaned closer. "You don't think it has anything to do with these parties, do you? That's all I've been able to think about since I've been here."

She glanced around. "I try not to pay attention, you know? I don't want to know what they're doing."

"It's probably safer that way."

She nodded. "Yeah, tell me about it. My brother has always said that Billy is trouble. I didn't tell him I was doing this."

"You've never felt like you're in danger, right?" I felt the need to step into a big-sister role.

She shrugged, but the action took just long enough that I was uncomfortable.

"Not really. I mean, some of the men are a little aggressive."

"Then why do you keep doing it?"

"Billy pays well. And it seems innocent enough. As long as I make good choices, you know?"

"I guess."

She studied me a minute. "You're really in

this area researching?"

"That's my story, and I'm sticking to it."

"Could I steal you away for a minute?" someone said behind me.

I looked over and saw the dark blond from earlier, the one who'd tried to put me in my place. I thought his name was Rupert.

"One second," I told him before leaning closer to Amy. "If you ever feel like you're in danger, get out of here. There are other things you can do to make money. Do you understand?"

She quickly nodded. "Yeah. Yeah. Totally. Of course."

Then she slipped back inside, leaving me out here with Rupert.

"I was hoping you and I might take a walk," he said. "On the beach."

No way, Jose. "It's a little cold for that."

Something gleaned in his eyes. "I'll keep you warm."

"I prefer one of these heaters." I could tell this guy wasn't going to take no easily. Fear crept in again.

His hand encircled my bicep. "It's just a walk. Don't freak out on me."

I refused to budge. "We can talk right here."

"But I don't want to talk right here." His words slurred. He'd been drinking too much.

I felt more uncomfortable than a conservative in Hollywood. "No alone time allowed. It's in my contract."

"Oh, come on. I hear you like to have fun." His grip on my arm tightened.

Panic flashed through me. What was I going to do if he didn't take no for an answer?

CHAPTER 12

"Leave her alone," someone said behind me.

I looked back and saw . . . Zane? What was he doing here? And wearing such an un-Zane outfit at that? Nice jeans, a rich-looking pink sweater, and loafers instead of flip-flops.

Rupert scowled but let go of my arm. "Your loss."

He turned and wandered back inside, muttering something I couldn't understand beneath his breath.

I turned to Zane. "Boy, am I glad to see you. What are you doing here?"

"I figured someone had to keep an eye on you. I'm all for women being independent and all, but I just couldn't stomach the thought of you being here alone."

Relief flushed through me, and I nearly fell into his arms. "Thanks, Zane."

"There are a lot of troublemakers here, Joey." He glanced around, his body strangely tense.

"Yeah, I've gathered that." I shivered again

and pulled my shawl closer. Not even the large outdoor heater above me was doing the trick.

"And not very many men who respect women for being people. They mostly respect women for being women, if you get my drift."

I thought I did. "Cora was here, Zane."

Zane shifted. "What are you hoping to find out about her? You really think these guys are going to help you?"

"I don't think they're going to help me on purpose. But I've got to figure out a way to find more information."

He let out a slow breath. "Well, I'm here. I've got your back."

Speaking of back . . . his hand rested on my lower back, on the exposed skin there, and all I could feel was fire.

I liked laid-back Zane a lot. But protective Zane had a lot going for him also.

We stepped back inside, and I gathered the lay of the land again. Across the room, I spotted Siegfried emerging from the hallway. Another man joined him, and the two surveyed the room.

"I need to talk to him," I whispered.

"You want me to come?"

I remembered the man's greeting when I'd arrived and decided I would be better off alone. "I'll call you if I need you."

"I'll be here."

With that, I sauntered over. I quickly observed the two men. Siegfried looked flashy and arrogant. But his friend had almost a nerdy look to him. Maybe it was his sweater vest or oversized glasses. He just didn't seem to fit in here though.

"Hello, boys," I greeted them.

Siegfried's eyes lit again. "Hello again, beautiful."

"Are you enjoying the party?"

He raised his eyebrows. "Anywhere you are is a good place to be."

I forced a giggle, even though I hated myself for it. Men like him shouldn't be encouraged. He was sleazy like Rupert, but also haughty with a god complex.

I glanced behind him. "And who are you?"

The man shifted awkwardly and extended his hand. "I'm Ryan."

"He's my brother." Siegfried raised his bottle.

That was when I noticed the dirt beneath his fingernails. Someone as meticulous as Siegfried wouldn't have dirt on his hands. My curiosity sparked, but I held it at bay. Fishing for answers might only end up with me being drowned.

I widened my eyes. "Your brother? Is that right? It's good to see brothers that remain such good friends."

"I'm enjoying some time off work, so I decided to accompany him here." Ryan shoved his hands into his pockets and appeared bored.

"Makes sense then."

Someone across the room motioned for Siegfried, and he excused himself. I heard the men begin a rousing conversation about a golf game they were planning on Monday as they walked away. That was when I turned to Ryan, hoping to get more information.

"You come to stuff like this often?"

He shrugged. "Not really. It's more Siegfried's scene than mine."

"How long have you been in town?"

"Ten days. On business."

That put them here at last week's party. They could have met Cora.

I looked at Siegfried. "He seems domineering."

"He's always been a go-getter. What can I say. I'm the one who loves numbers and planning. He's the one who'll put himself out there."

Ryan seemed like the most down-to-earth person to get information from. With that thought in mind, I pulled out Cora's picture from my clutch. "Have you seen this girl, by chance?"

His eyes widened, and he looked away. "She

looks vaguely familiar. Why?"

"She's missing."

"And you're asking me because?"

"She was at one of these parties."

He pressed his lips together, as if in deep thought. "I thought you were supposed to be a hostess here. You sound like you're a private eye."

"I'm just asking questions."

"Well, if you don't mind, I should go." He nodded toward his brother. "Take care."

As he sauntered away, Zane joined me. My insides were wound tighter than Scarlett O'Hara's corset.

"Did you find out anything?" Zane asked.

"I'm not sure."

Zane stiffened as Billy started toward us. "Play along," Zane whispered.

"Zane, you decided to come after all. What brought the change of heart?"

Zane wrapped his arm around me. "Do you need to ask?"

"That's what I figured," Billy said. "I'd keep an eye on Joey if she was my girl too. I'm still not sure why she's here exactly."

"I told you. Research."

He rolled his eyes. "You do a lot of researching."

"Most people only see the glamorous part of my job. They don't see the behind the scenes."

"Well, the guys are happy you're here, so I guess there's no harm, no foul. But if you talk to anyone about anything that's happened here tonight, I'll cut your fingers off one by one."

I sucked in a breath.

Then Billy started to laugh.

"Just joking. Of course. Have fun, you two."

I exchanged a glance with Zane. All his laid-back surfer vibes were disappearing faster than eroding shoreline in a hurricane.

"We should get out of here," Zane said.

"I still don't know anything," I whispered back. "I'm under contract to stay for at least two hours. I have no idea what happened here that may have gotten Cora killed."

"Probably what's going on in that room," Zane said, nodding down the hallway.

"What's going on there?"

"You stay here, and I'll find out."

I grabbed his arm. "I don't want to pull you into this."

"I'll be fine." He leaned closer and kissed my cheek. "I promise."

He strutted to the back hallway, and I lifted up a prayer. *Let him be okay. Please.*

Just as he disappeared from sight, the front

door burst open.

Police invaded the house like ants on a slice of watermelon.

And Jackson Sullivan stood in the midst of them, staring at me with an expression of disbelief on his face.

CHAPTER 13

Officers swarmed through the house, along with another detective holding a warrant in his hand. The music had ended, leaving the place feeling deflated and empty. The strobe lights were off, and glaring overhead lights were on.

And Zane was still nowhere to be seen.

"What in the world are you doing here?" Jackson stared at me as I crossed my arms in the corner—the area I'd gravitated to when the commotion started.

"No, the question is: What are you doing here?" If in doubt, turn the tables. My favorite piece of advice yet.

"I'm doing my job. There was a notice about underage drinking here."

"Underage? Who?"

He nodded in the distance, and I saw the other detective talking to Amy. Billy stood beside them, exclaiming, "She told me she was twenty-one!" Meanwhile, Amy shrugged as if she couldn't care less.

"We've been keeping our eyes on these parties for a while," Jackson said, lowering his voice and sidling beside me, no doubt so he could have a view of the room as well.

"Why?"

A hand went to his hip. "I'm the one asking questions here, Joey. Since you're here, maybe you need to go down to the station as well."

I raised my hands, not wanting to go through that again. Once was enough. "I didn't do anything wrong."

"There's nothing good happening here. Nothing." He sliced a hand through the air.

I swallowed hard, looking around once more for Zane. I hoped he didn't get in trouble because of me. One of the men I'd seen earlier was led away in handcuffs, shouting profanities as he went.

"There's an arrest warrant out for him," Jackson said. "Not only did he embezzle money from his company, but as he was spending thus-said money, he hit a man with his car and fled the scene. We've been trying to track him down for a while now."

"I see." They'd been looking for an excuse to bust this joint. Amy had given them the ammunition they needed.

"They're not great people to be around."

"Cora was at one of these parties last week," I blurted.

"So you thought it was a good idea if you came also?"

"No, in my defense, I never thought this was a good idea. It was just my *only* idea."

His cheeks puffed out, as if all his frustration built up pressure inside him and neared explosion. Finally, he slowly released the air. Shut his eyes. Opened them again. Purposefully. Methodically. Perfectly in control.

"What's it going to take to get through to you, Joey? You've already almost been killed more than once. Do you think you're invincible?"

My cheeks stung as if I'd been slapped. "Nothing happened here, Jackson. My life isn't in danger. I was just at a party."

I remembered Rupert and shivered. This could have turned ugly if Zane hadn't arrived when he did.

Jackson leaned closer. "Drugs. Gambling. People who are risk takers. Who think they're invincible. Who think women are objects. That's who's here tonight."

He had a point. This was a terrible idea.

"I only wanted to help," I finally said. How many times was I going to say that?

"You can help by staying out of it.

Understand?"

I nodded. "I understand."

Before Jackson could change his mind and possibly actually take me down to the station, I found Zane and left.

***

"I'm still not sure I understand," I told Zane once we were back at my duplex.

"Those guys are up to no good. They live fast and furious, and they don't care who gets in the way."

"But who are they? I don't understand that party scene. They're not college kids. They're grown men." I paced in my living room, trying to sort my thoughts out.

Zane stopped me by gripping my arms as we stood face to face. "Those guys who attend those parties think they own the world. They're rich. They're successful. And they feel untouchable."

I got that. But something still didn't make sense. "Okay . . . but why the parties?"

"I suppose they don't feel like any of the nightlife in this area is suitable for someone with their stature."

"Really? That's pretty presumptuous."

Zane released me and put his hands on his

hips. "Billy charges a fee for them to come. It's discreet. They network. They party. They meet girls. If anyone gets out of line, they face consequences."

"What kind?"

"One guy I know had his face rearranged."

All the moisture left my throat. "What was going on in that back room? I thought I was going to get you arrested."

"Gambling. Some marijuana."

That wasn't good. It wasn't good at all. "Zane, how do you know these guys?"

He ran a hand over his eyes and stepped back. Laid-back Zane was nowhere to be seen. "I haven't always done things I'm proud of, Joey."

"One of the men there was a wanted criminal!"

"I know, okay?"

"He embezzled money, and he was involved in a hit-and-run."

He jerked his eyes open and locked gazes with me. "Joey, I wouldn't have gone if you hadn't been there. You know that, right?"

I nodded, more confused than ever. "Yeah, I guess I do."

He took my hand and kissed my fingers. "I didn't want to see anything happen to you."

"I appreciate that. Truly."

"I introduced you to Billy, and I'll never forgive myself if you get tangled in his net."

Tangled in his net? I envisioned a mermaid, caught and unable to get away.

And that was when I knew I couldn't drop this.

CHAPTER 14

"You look distracted," Dizzy said.

It was just my luck that today was another extremely slow day at the salon. I needed to stay busy to distract myself from my heavy thoughts. So far, I'd organized shampoo. Counted my tip jar. Mopped the floor. Now I was painting my nails a lovely teal.

"I had a rough night." I had circles under my eyes. A high bun because I didn't feel like fixing my hair. And even though my outfit was decent, I still felt slouchy.

Too many things raced through my mind. Things like Billy's party. Jackson bursting in. The rounds of questions afterward.

The new realization that Jackson hated me again.

We seemed to keep doing this dance. Get close. Get on his bad side. Pull away. Get close again.

It was enough to make my head spin. And I hated the fact that I even cared.

"What happened?" Dizzy sat down across from me and fanned her face as "Blue Christmas" played overhead.

"I decided to go to a party Billy Corbina was hosting so I could find out information about something," I admitted, stroking the brush across my fingernail but hitting a cuticle instead.

"Any party that Billy has can't be a good one."

I had a feeling that Dizzy and her friends could match their craziness, just in a different way.

I frowned and used another nail to wipe the polish from my cuticle. "It wasn't. The police came. Said it was about underage drinking, but I think they secretly suspected that a drug deal was going on."

"Was there some brown sugar? Crank? Speckled birds?"

I froze from my manicure. "How do you know those street names?"

She shrugged. "I watched *Breaking Bad*."

I just couldn't see her watching that show, but I nodded. "Anyway, nothing going on there seemed on the up and up."

She continued to fan herself. "I'm surprised Billy let you go. He usually keeps his inner circle pretty close."

"I guess I am too." I blew on my nails, trying

to forget everything that had happened, including the disappointment on Jackson's face that I had been part of such a scene.

"Did you discover anything for your investigation, at least?"

I let out a deep breath. "It's hard to say. I confirmed that the missing girl had been there last week. Did she overhear something about some drug deals that got her killed? Did something else happen? I don't know."

"I thought it was the photographer in the preserve with the ... camera?" She shrugged. "I was trying to make it sound like the game of Clue."

I turned my chair left and right. Left and right. "I think he's clear. He's a con artist, and maybe he should be in jail. But we don't think he hurt Cora. His alibi checked out. He met a girl for drinks right after his session with Cora."

"So where does this leave you?"

I shrugged "I have no idea. I had a clue from the 7-Eleven where Cora stopped. The guy working there saw a beat-up white pickup outside. Cora was arguing with the driver. I can be certain that no one at the party last night would dare sink as low as to drive a beat-up truck like that."

"I see."

"Cora also purchased an umbrella stand. The photographer said there was no umbrella in their session. So why did she stop and buy one?"

"Good question."

"I'm not ready to drop what happened at Billy's. I just don't know how to prove anything illegal there—unless sleaziness is outlawed. Something definitely wasn't on the up and up."

"Oh, you'll figure it out, Joey. I just know you will."

Cora had been missing for six days. Every day the likelihood that we would find her diminished more and more. I wished that she would just pop up somewhere and admit that she'd taken off on a crazy whim. I had wished the same thing about my father, but that hadn't come to fruition.

I'd promised Elrod I would help. And I planned on doing just that.

***

As I normally did, I went on my lunch break to Oh Buoy. The place was hopping today, so I didn't have time to talk to Phoebe. I grabbed a corner booth and sat with my back to the rest of the building.

This was a no-no for professional law enforcement. Raven had taught me that. You should always sit where you could watch people and get a feel for who was coming and going.

Today I wanted to be alone and block out the world.

Which might have been fine if someone didn't slide in across from me. I'd hoped it might be Phoebe, but I was sadly mistaken.

It was Billy Corbina.

I swallowed hard and tried to stay as cool as my Coquina Crush. "Billy. Wasn't expecting to see you here."

"Where'd you think I'd be? Jail?"

In this light I could clearly see a scar at his temple. I'd never noticed it before. Of course, I usually saw him in dark, distasteful places.

"I didn't say that," I told him.

"Were you at my party last night as part of a setup?"

Sweat tried to break out across my forehead. "No, the police knew nothing about it."

He narrowed his eyes. "Because I heard you're working with them now."

"Working with them would be a stretch. I'm just doing research."

"You do a lot of research."

"I take my roles very seriously. Do you think it's easy looking that super-intelligent?" *What did I just say?*

Amusement flashed in his eyes.

"Besides, do you think Jackson Sullivan is going to let me anywhere close to one of his investigations? He hates me. He'd trust a parolee faster than he'd trust me handling a sensitive case."

Billy let out a deep chuckle that ended abruptly with a threatening stare. "What project is this for?"

"It's all hush-hush. I'm under contract." Under contract with myself. That wasn't an important detail to share.

He leaned closer. "I don't like where this is going."

"Where what is going?" I totally agreed with the sentiment, and apprehension slithered through me. As "Don't Worry, Be Happy" rang out on the overhead, I wished the reggae number rang true in my life.

He leaned toward me, that tiger-hunting-its-prey look flashing in his eyes again. "I think you're up to something."

I drew in a deep breath. *Think like Raven, Joey. Think like Raven. Remain cool. In control. Unflappable.* That was when I decided to turn the tables. "The real question is: What are you up to, Billy?"

His gaze still looked cool as he leaned back.

"I've been conducting my business in this area for a long time. Much longer than you've been around town. I don't intend to stop."

By business, I was pretty sure he didn't mean Willie Wahoo's. "Describe your business."

His eyes narrowed. "That's none of yours. Let's just say there are people who come to this area for a good time, and I give it to them. Nothing illegal about it."

He wasn't the only one with pressing questions. I leveled my gaze with him. "What do you know about Cora Day, the girl who disappeared from Nags Head Woods? I know she was at one of your parties."

His face went a little paler. "I don't know what you're talking about."

"I think you do." I wasn't letting him off that hook that easily.

"Anyone who comes to my shindigs comes on their own free will."

"Maybe she came by her own free will. But what happened while she was there? Did things go south?"

His gaze cooled even more. "You're a little troublemaker, aren't you?"

"You're avoiding the question."

"All I know is that she left in a hurry. Didn't even say goodbye."

"What happened before she left?"

"She was just talking to some guys."

That was a start. "Which ones?"

"I'm not at liberty to say."

"Of course you're not." I may or may not have rolled my eyes at that one.

Billy leaned closer, animosity gleaming in his eyes. "You need to stay away from this. Stay away from my parties. I know where to find you, Joey."

I shivered in my fake-bamboo seat. That was clearly a threat. "What happens if I don't?"

"You don't want to know."

CHAPTER 15

I found Zane after I got off work. He was beneath the duplex, hard at work restoring an old surfboard. He had curls of . . . some substance I couldn't identify . . . stuck to his shirt, a sheen of sweat across his shoulders, and the very attractive look of concentration on his face.

Until he saw me.

Then his face lit up like the red carpet at the Oscars. He put his planing tool down and turned toward me.

"Hey, Joey!"

"Nice-looking board." And it was. It had a retro vibe to it, with dark-brown sides and a deep-orange stripe down the middle.

"Isn't she a beaut? I call her the Daytona. This girl has seen more waves in her lifetime than me and all my surfing buddies combined."

"You working on it for a client?"

Zane nodded. "That's right. There's a lot of joy in fixing these girls up. With her history, there's no way she should become a wall hanging at some rental house. No, she's still got some years left in her."

"I'm glad you can help with her makeover then."

"Speaking of being glad . . . I'm glad you're here. I have a question for you."

"What's that?" I leaned against the door of the outside shower. Colors of the sunset smeared in the distance, and the temperature had noticeably dropped, making me wish I had a sweatshirt.

"What in the world am I supposed to wear to the movie premiere? I need to get a tux, right? Any special kind of tux?"

I quickly reviewed our last conversation in my mind. I couldn't remember confirming that he was going with me to the premiere of *Family Secrets*. Had I? He seemed pretty assured he was.

So I must have given him that impression, and I supposed that was fine. It was better than going alone. Especially since Eric would be there.

"You're coming?" I clarified.

"Oh yeah. Of *course*. I wouldn't miss it for the world." He twisted his head. "Did I misunderstand? Didn't you invite me? Because if I got the wrong impression, I totally get it. Don't feel like I have to go."

I tried to replay our conversation again.

"I've got to plan our next undertaking," Zane

had said.

"It will have to be after my movie premiere."
He'd raised his eyebrows. "Or will it?"

"I must have only half been paying attention. And of course I'd love for you to come. Tuxes are a must. We can get you one when we get to LA though. You don't want to travel with it."

He rubbed the side of his surfboard. "Smart thinking. I'm so excited. I think this will be a lot of fun."

"Yeah, totally." I perched myself on a bench in front of him. "I have a question for you also."

He brushed his hand across the board before coming to sit beside me. "What's going on?"

"I know you told me that the guys at the parties are no good. But you also said you were invited to one of those parties. What's your association?"

"Like I told you, Billy and I went to high school together. We were close. We're not anymore. But he still likes to remember me as I used to be."

I didn't have to ask Zane, but I knew the truth. Zane had a drug problem as a teen, and Billy had been a part of that scene. No doubt there were a lot of bad memories there.

"I need to figure out who those guys are, Zane," I said. "One of them may know what happened to Cora. Her life could be in danger."

He flicked a shaving curl off his shirt. "What if she just ran away? Ran off to Hollywood to try and make it big? What if there's no foul play here at all?"

"There was blood. You saw it."

"She could have cut herself. Walking barefoot maybe?"

"But what if she didn't? What if she's in trouble? I have the potential to do something to help her. I plan on doing that. I don't understand why you're giving me so much opposition. What happened to your bucket list? To your hashtag adventures?"

He ran a hand through his hair.

I leaned forward. "You know I'm doing it with or without you, right?"

"Yeah, I know that." He let out another sigh. "One of his guys is Rupert Murphy. He's the one who was hitting on you when I got to the party."

"What do you know about this Rupert guy?"

"I met him at a surfing competition. Billy hosted a party afterward. I don't know him well, but I know he has a lot of money. Not sure where he gets it. He has a house here and also one up in New Jersey, I think. He drives fast cars, he loves women, and he's fearless."

"Where can I find this guy?"

Zane pressed his lips together a moment, as if contemplating how much to say. Finally, he looked at me. "There's a back room at Willie's for VIP customers. He usually hangs out there."

***

There was no way I was going into Willie's again, not after my conversation with Billy earlier today. Instead, I sat in the parking lot, watching from the safety of my Miata and waiting for something to happen.

The bad news was that my red Mazda Miata stood out in this parking lot like Lady Gaga at a Christian music festival. The good news was that I wasn't alone.

Zane sat beside me, eating peanuts again. Apparently one of his real estate clients from Virginia had given him a big bag of fresh-from-the-earth squirrel food. He had eating them down to a science. *Crack the shell open. Use shell like a holder. Cock head back. Flop peanuts into mouth. Repeat.*

Darkness had fallen. Music from the inside blared out through the nearly nonexistent windows in the place—never a good sign for a restaurant if there were no windows. In my experience, at least. People went in looking normal and left laughing too hard and staggering off balance.

"What are you going to do if and when Rupert comes out?" Zane placed his discarded shells in a plastic bag.

"Follow him." I'd already decided that.

"And then what?"

"I have no idea," I said. "If he goes home, I can't exactly go inside after him."

"No, you can't."

"There are a lot of variables here." I'd tried to think through several scenarios, but I knew what I did best—or worst, depending on who asked. I played it by ear.

A moment of silence stretched between us.

Zane leaned back and attempted to stretch his long legs in the cramped space. He'd worn his favorite ripped jeans and a yellow sweatshirt with *Slick Ocean* across the front. "Any more word from your super stalker fan club?"

That was what I'd started calling the group of somewhat extreme fans. It all began back in LA with one man named Leonard. I'd gotten a restraining order against him, and he'd seemed to have disappeared.

Until I came here to the Outer Banks.

Then he popped up again. And he had an accomplice who still remained faceless.

Then it turned out there were more than two. In fact, there was a whole little club of people who considered themselves fans, and they operated a site on the dark web. Also, apparently, they liked to post my schedule to make it easier for other stalkers who wanted to make my life miserable.

"No, they've been strangely quiet lately." I took a sip of my coffee. I'd stopped by my favorite place, Sunrise Coffee Co., on the way here. Priorities.

"Quiet is good, right?"

"Sometimes the quiet is suspicious." Because I was sure they were still out there and still watching. Probably planning and plotting their next attempt to keep Raven Remington alive.

Jackson had opened a file on them, but so far the police had no luck tracking anyone down. It was all weird, almost like these guys were professionals. Professional stalkers? I shuddered just thinking about it. But how else had they eluded authorities? Eluded me? And they always seemed to know what was going on. It was all very strange.

Zane elbowed me and sat up. "Believe it or not, that's Rupert right there. He's leaving Willie's."

I glanced at the time. It was only nine. This

seemed early to wrap up an evening for a jet-setter like Rupert.

He didn't even glance at us as he walked—yes, he walked. Not stumbled or teetered or any other indication he'd had too much to drink—over to his Mercedes. He climbed inside, slammed the door, and cranked the engine.

Mine was already cranked and ready to go.

I slowly crept out behind him, careful not to lose him. I eased onto the highway and stayed a safe distance behind. He pulled up to an abandoned storefront located just off the main highway. I sidled into an adjoining gas station parking lot and turned the car off.

"That's the old laser-tag building," Zane said. "My friends and I used to love going there, but it's been closed for probably a decade."

"Interesting." I opened my door.

"What are you doing?" Zane asked.

"I've got to see what he's up to." Before Zane could argue with me, I hopped out. I'd been smart enough to wear all black so I could blend in. Zane, on the other hand, would stand out like sunshine on a cloudy day in his yellow sweatshirt.

He caught up with me in two strides.

"You don't have to come," I whispered, hurrying across the asphalt.

"Like I'm going to let you do this alone."

I rushed over the grassy median between the gas station and abandoned laser-tag building. "You're not really dressed for this job."

He glanced down at his shirt. "Then I'll be sure to stay out of sight."

Zane stayed on my heels as I rushed toward the vinyl-encased building. Rupert had pulled up at the other side. Even from where I was, I could hear someone talking in the distance.

"This will be the perfect place to keep her," a man said in the distance.

I exchanged a look with Zane.

Her? As in Cora?

"No, no one knows why I'm here," the same voice said. "Of course. I'm smarter than that."

Rupert must be talking on the phone, because I couldn't hear any responses. I was thankful that the darkness concealed us. There were no overhead lights on this building.

"No, I promise," he continued. "We'll be good to go by next week. Everything will be taken care of."

Everything will be taken care of? Was he going to kill Cora? What if she was in that building right now?

I heard something rattling and then a slam. Had he gone inside?

His voice disappeared.

Zane's eyes met mine. "What do you want to do now?"

My fingers dug into the cool metal covering the building. It had turned surprisingly cold outdoors, and my leather jacket wasn't cutting it. "I want to wait until he leaves. And then I want to check out that building."

Zane rested a hand on my arm. "I don't say this very often, but maybe we should call the police."

His words snapped me out of my She-Ra stupor. Charging forward on my own would do no good right now. In fact, it would probably get someone hurt—either me or Cora. I didn't want to put Cora at risk.

"You're probably right. It would be the smart thing to do." I pulled out my cell phone and dialed Jackson's number.

He didn't answer. Strange. He always answered when I called. I hadn't realized it, but I'd come to count on Jackson being available.

But I wouldn't be deterred. I called Loose Lips Danny instead.

"Danny, it's Joey Darling," I whispered. "I may have found the missing girl, Cora Day."

"Where are you?" he asked.

I told him.

"Lay low," Danny said. "We're on our way."

CHAPTER 16

"I want to see what he's doing," I whispered.

"We should wait for the police."

Just then, something screeched. Metal. The door, I realized. Was Rupert coming back out?

Zane touched my arm, sending my nerves scrambling. "If he leaves, we have a better chance of helping Cora. We just have to be patient and not blow it."

He was right. But it took every ounce of self-control to remain where I was.

Footsteps sounded. A car door opened and closed. An engine started.

Rupert was leaving.

"Hide!" I whispered, realizing he would come right past us.

We darted around the opposite corner and ducked behind an old trash can there. A moment later, Rupert pulled away. When he was out of sight, we rose. As we did, two police cars pulled up.

I hoped to see Jackson. But it was Danny and

another officer. Duck Donuts.

"We think Cora is inside," I told them.

"Why do you think that?" Danny rested his hand on his belt.

"Because that's what it sounded like. This guy Rupert was talking on his phone to someone." I recounted what he'd said.

Danny looked at Duck Donuts. "Do we need a warrant?"

"Maybe we should wait for Detective Harrison?" Duck Donuts said.

"Every minute counts here," I told him, my muscles wound entirely too tightly.

"You're right." Loose Lips found a bolt cutter in his trunk and cut the padlock off the back door.

I held my breath as they pulled the door opened and went inside.

I knew I was supposed to stand down, but I couldn't help but creep closer to the opening. I desperately wanted to know if Cora was inside.

Instead, I saw . . . a car?

"Cora's not here." Loose Lips stomped back outside.

"That can't be right. Rupert said this would be the perfect place to keep her." I'd been so sure he'd find her.

"He was talking about his cars," Danny said. "I

just made a call. He's hoping to open a luxury car dealership here. He has to have the paperwork done by next week. He's going to showcase his limited-edition Bugatti Veyron by Mansory Vivere."

"His what?"

"His three-million-dollar car," Danny said.

I wanted to bury my face. The one time I try to be responsible, and I only ended up humiliated. Wasn't that just great?

I shrugged. "At least I called."

***

"That's quite the article you have in the *Instigator*," Dizzy said the next morning at work.

"What do you mean?" I didn't even want to ask. The *Instigator* had published some horrible stuff about me. Ninety-five percent of it wasn't true, and the five percent that was true was mostly about my cellulite.

And right now I had an audience at Beach Combers. Dizzy's friends MaryAnn, Geraldine, and Maxine had stopped by for a quick visit. The place was officially closed for lunch, so the ladies had brought cupcakes, of all things. I loved cupcakes, but they weren't on my diet unless they were made with coconut flour and stevia.

Of course I couldn't resist eating one though.

I grabbed the one with the tallest pile of creamy icing, swiped a glop of chocolate buttercream onto my finger, and indulged for a moment in the ooey, gooey goodness.

"You haven't seen it yet?" Maxine asked.

"I probably don't want to." I had to learn to ignore what the *Instigator* said and to stop reading those headlines. They only served to mess up my mental space.

Despite my words, Dizzy plopped the rag mag into my lap. There on the cover was a picture of me. Two pictures of me, for that matter. One with Zane and the other with Jackson.

I suddenly forgot about my cupcake. I set it on my station and picked up the publication. The picture of Zane and me showed us laughing together. I was giggling so hard I'd thrown my head back. His hand was at my waist, and we both stood on the beach, looking like the picture of happiness.

The next picture was of me with Jackson. We were at the photo shoot with Andre. I was wearing that mermaid costume, and Jackson had helped me up after my face-plant into the sand. Helping me up was a little bit of an understatement. His very capable arms were beneath my knees and shoulders. My arms were around his neck.

From the outside looking in, we appeared like we'd been caught in a romantic moment. Little did people know that Jackson was only minutes away from grilling me about investigating Cora's disappearance on my own.

However, both pictures were taken totally out of context.

The headline below read: *Joey Darling Juggles Two Hunks. Whom Will She Choose?*

I closed my eyes. Jackson was going to *love* that. And that was sarcasm, in case you were wondering.

On the other hand, Zane really might love it. And that wasn't sarcasm, in case you were wondering.

How had the paparazzi gotten these pictures? I hadn't even seen anyone out there on either of those days. Was I that oblivious to both my stalkers and the paparazzi? Absolutely.

"It looks like you've got your hands full," Maxine said.

I sighed and pulled my gaze away from the pictures. "Not really. I'm not dating either. We're just friends."

She held up another copy of the *Instigator*. "Could have fooled us."

I leaned back and decided to give my full

attention to the cupcake again. After all, cupcakes had never broken my heart. They'd never published lies about me. They'd never hurt me—unless body fat counted. "Like I said, we're just friends. But this is what I don't understand. Should you be with someone who's just like you or be with someone who's your opposite?" I glanced around. "All of you have been married. What do you think?"

"Opposite, for sure."

"Just like you, definitely."

"In between, if you ask me."

"There's no easy answer."

I wanted to bury my head. They all had different responses. Of course.

When I'd been married to Eric, I'd thought he was my opposite. He was suave and sophisticated, and he understood the acting business. He'd already made films and developed connections and seemed to have a handle on both his money and his fame.

But after we were married, I'd realized that none of that was real. He was uneven and temperamental and brooding. Our moments of happiness were really happy, but our low moments were really low. And it seemed like the low moments kept coming more and more frequently until that was all we had together.

Low eventually morphed into violence.

I'd never before doubted my abilities with men so much. I'd also began to doubt my own instincts. I'd gotten it totally wrong with Eric. I wouldn't do that again.

"No offense, but y'all are no help," I said apologetically.

"You can't choose between the two of them?" MaryAnn asked.

"It's not that Zane or Jackson is asking me to choose. But if I had to, I have no idea what I'd do. Do I choose the thrill-seeking adventurer? The one whom life would never be boring with? The one who's like the waves he loves so much? Or do I choose the steady one who makes me feel safe? Who's always been noble and pure? The rock?"

"The wave or the rock," Dizzy repeated. "That is a dilemma. We should test that theory out with the Romeos."

"Who are the Romeos?" I asked.

Dizzy grinned. "You'll have to meet them sometime. It stands for Retired Old Men Eating Out. We like to get together sometimes. While eating out. Of course."

I had so many questions about this, but before I could ask, my phone rang. It was Jackson.

I quickly excused myself as the ladies hooted and hollered in the background like a bunch of middle school students.

"Listen, I don't know what you're doing, but I need to unwind," he said. "I'm taking the boat out fishing. You want to come along?"

"Really?" I'd thought he'd want to wipe his hands clean of me. "When?"

"This afternoon around three or so. The weather is good, the water is good, and I need a break."

"Sounds good. I'll meet you at your place?"

"I'll see you then."

CHAPTER 17

"All right, are you ready for this?" Jackson asked, standing at the pier with Ripley on one side of him and his boat bobbing on the other side.

"Am I ever." I held up a cooler as I approached him on the long stretch of plank. "I even brought dinner."

He paused from rolling up a rope. "You made something?"

I did a half snort, half laugh. "Of course not. I picked it up from the sandwich shop."

"That works too."

I glanced at the boat. "So this is *Escape*?"

"That's right. It's usually only when I'm out here on the water that I feel like I can get away."

The boat wasn't small or large. It could probably hold six people. It had a bench at the back and a seat at the console, where Jackson would steer the boat. Jackson hopped on board, and Ripley followed behind him.

Jackson seemed so laid back right now. He

wore jeans and a sweatshirt and a baseball cap. The weather was balmy, and I'd donned my favorite hoodie—it was bright pink—and jeans.

He reached out his hand toward me. "I'll help you on."

I took his hand, ignoring the volt of electricity I felt. Again, I was acting as nervous as Bambi during hunting season. Why was I always so nervous around him?

I mean, I wasn't like this around Zane. I always felt comfortable around him. I felt like I could be myself. There was a lot to be said for that.

On the other hand, Jackson always left me feeling unbalanced.

I stepped into the boat. Once I had my footing, I lowered myself onto the little bench at the back, noting the fishing poles and tackle box.

For a moment, I was transported back to my childhood. I remembered doing stuff like this with my dad. The simple days. I missed them. I wanted them. But life didn't work like that. I was a living and breathing testament to that fact.

"I heard you had some excitement last night," Jackson said, easing the boat away from the dock. Ripley ran toward the bow and took his place there, looking like he'd done this a million times before.

"False excitement." I frowned, remembering how everything had unfolded.

I might have felt embarrassed, but I was focusing too much on the realization that Jackson hadn't been there. And that seemed unusual. In fact, it had been bothering me ever since then. Which was silly.

Just because he was a detective didn't mean he had to be on call all the time. Certainly he liked to shut his phone off and have a life outside of police work sometimes. Maybe he'd even had plans on a Friday night.

After a few minutes of silence, I said, "You should be proud. I tried to call you."

"I was proud. Good job, Joey."

We cruised deeper into the sound. Finally Jackson slowed, anchoring the boat, and grabbed a fishing rod.

Er . . . he still wasn't offering any details. And that was a crying shame.

"I guess you don't work twenty-four seven like I thought," I said, practicing my fishing skills by angling for answers.

He handed me a pole. "I guess I do have a few surprises up my sleeve."

"I'm trying to figure out what you might have been doing if not working. Let me guess: taxes."

He smiled ever so slightly. "Nope."

Was he enjoying this?

"Playing cards?" I continued, unable to drop this.

"Not really my thing."

"Taking a moonlight walk with Ripley?"

"Nope. And you have no faith that I'm capable of doing things beyond taxes and moonlit walks?"

"I didn't mean that . . ." Only I had. Kind of. I'd made him sound like he could be one of the Romeos. "Fine, I'm done."

He chuckled. "I thought you'd be more persistent than that."

"Well, even I know my limits."

He finished prepping his fishing rod, and I fiddled with mine as well, making sure the line was wound and threaded correctly.

"I was actually out on a date," Jackson said.

My heartbeat was suddenly localized to my ears. A date? Why did that bother me? It shouldn't bother me. Not onc bit. But no wonder the man didn't answer his phone. The last thing he'd want would be to hear from me while romancing someone else.

"Someone at church fixed me up," Jackson continued.

"Well, that sounds like a nice evening then."

He shrugged. "Not really. I'm not actually that

great at dating."

"But you've been married before."

"With Claire it came easy. We didn't really date. We just hit it off and knew that we were supposed to be together."

"That's very sweet." I shifted. "Does that mean there won't be a second date?"

"It's very unlikely."

"I'm sure you're better at dating than you think you are."

"I'm not so sure about that. The kicker came when she took my phone from me."

My eyes widened, but I tried to conceal it by grabbing a worm from the tub and placing it on the hook. "Your date took your cell phone? On your first date?"

He nodded. "Yeah, she said she'd had some bad experiences on first dates before and hated feeling second fiddle to technology."

I resisted the urge to snort. "Did you ask for it back?"

"Of course. She refused. I decided to play along—but only for an hour. Then if I had to go into her purse myself, I would."

I pictured the scene taking place and felt halfway amused and halfway horrified. With the image of someone snatching Jackson's phone still firmly in my mind, I stared out at the water, glad

I was fishing and not dealing with dating drama.

"I think I'm finally getting the hang of this." I cast my line into the water again.

"Don't get too cocky."

"Never." I let out a contented sigh and watched as the sun set in the background. "It feels so serene out here."

Jackson followed my gaze. "Doesn't it, though? I could sit out here watching every sunset every night and be perfectly satisfied."

"I think I have something!" I began reeling my line in, excited to see if I'd actually caught a fish.

Jackson reached around me, helping me.

"Keep it steady," he murmured.

Nothing was steady when his arms were around me. Yet at the same time, everything was steady.

Finally, the line broke the surf. I held my breath, waiting to see what I'd caught.

A plastic bag full of water emerged.

"Would you look at that?" Jackson released me and let out an amused chuckle.

"At least it wasn't a boot." I continued to reel it in.

"Well, on the bright side, maybe you just saved a sea turtle."

"You get sea turtles in the sound?"

"In the winter they'll come here for the

warmer waters sometimes. If I see one, I usually call the team over at the aquarium, just to make sure the turtle isn't injured or ill."

"That's so cool . . . that you've found sea turtles. Not that they could be ill or injured."

"Down on Hatteras, sometimes you can find nests near the dunes, and if you time it right, you'll see the babies hatch and scramble toward the sea. There's nothing like it."

"I can imagine." My hands were trembling. And it was all Jackson's fault. He made me nervous.

I sighed. Once I unhooked the plastic bag, I put down my rod. "Maybe I'll take a little break and just watch the sunset."

"Sounds like a plan."

We pulled out the sandwiches I'd brought and dug in. Quietly we sat side by side and watched the smear of colors on the horizon. The clouds seemed to have coordinated with the sun, and they splayed out, giving an even more robust picture of the sunset. It was a great way to say goodbye to the day.

Despite everything that had gone wrong, I felt happy at the moment. I actually couldn't remember the last time I felt happy. I remembered having fun. Being flattered. Feeling excited.

But I couldn't truly remember feeling content.

"You're rubbing your scar again," Jackson said quietly.

I looked down, and sure enough, I was rubbing it. I quickly moved my hand.

Silence stretched between us. Jackson wasn't audibly asking what happened. But I could sense he wanted to know.

I wasn't sure why my volatile relationship with Eric was on my mind. Unless it was because of Rupert. Rupert, who reminded me of Eric and who'd brought back so many memories. Sometimes it was the unexpected triggers that affected you the most. And in this case, it was definitely true.

Starla was the only one I'd ever talked to about the events of that day. No one else. Not the police. Not my dad. Not Zane.

I'd told Jackson before that it was from my car accident, but he didn't seem to believe me. It was like the man had a built-in lie detector.

And I didn't know why, but part of me wanted to tell Jackson the truth. He felt like someone who was safe to share it with.

"I fell down the stairs," I blurted before I could second-guess myself.

"I thought it was from a car accident."

My arm began trembling at the memories, and I stroked Ripley to conceal the reaction. "That's what I always tell people."

"Are you ashamed of falling down the stairs? Because it's happened to the best of us."

I continued to stare at the sunset. "Eric pushed me."

Jackson released a quick breath. "What?"

I nodded, unable to make eye contact with him. On the verge of changing my mind and claiming I was just joking. But I couldn't go back now.

"Our relationship was pretty volatile toward the end. I tried to talk to him about finances, but he'd been drinking. He wanted to shut me up, so he slapped me. I fell. Hit a vase on the way down. It shattered, and I cut myself."

"Joey . . . I had no idea." His voice sounded hoarse, soft, angry.

"No one does."

"Did you report him?"

I shook my head. "No."

"You should."

"It's water under the bridge now."

"Men like that shouldn't get away with abusing their power."

"You're right."

Jackson remained quiet a minute, and I could

tell he was ruminating on what I said. He shook his head and said, "Yet you were in a car accident, right?"

Memories flooded back like a dam that collapsed. "I passed out on the floor. When I woke up, I was in a pool of blood. Eric had taken my phone and left me there to deal with my injuries alone. I tried to drive myself to the hospital. Looking back, I should have probably gone to a neighbor's. But I was embarrassed. And horrified. And . . . so many other emotions."

"You never reported him?"

I shook my head. "It would have been front-page news. And there's always a certain amount of shame that comes with something like that. I just wanted to forget it happened. That's when I left Eric."

"Joey . . ." The word was full of emotion.

I still couldn't look at Jackson. I didn't want to see the pity in his eyes.

"I shouldn't have shared any of this." I shook my head again, desperately wishing I could hide. "I don't know why I did—"

He grabbed my hand and squeezed. "I'm glad you did. You don't have anything to be ashamed of. Eric should be in jail."

"I just want to put it behind me."

Jackson didn't say anything. He remained

quiet, but I could see him thinking. I could sense that he wasn't happy.

Almost hesitantly, he stood and walked toward the helm. Instantly I felt alone. Almost as if Jackson recognized that, he turned and extended his arm. "Come stand with me."

Intrigue rushed through me. "Are you sure?"

"Of course I'm sure."

I should have known. Jackson didn't do anything he wasn't sure about.

I joined him at the wheel. He placed his hand on my back to steady me.

And I realized just how appropriate that was. Jackson was always there to keep me grounded.

He pointed to a boat in the distance. "I can't be sure, but I think that person is taking pictures."

Anger flared in me. Paparazzi or stalkers?

I didn't know.

As if to answer us, gunfire rang out.

Apparently, it was neither. Also apparently, it was worse.

Someone was shooting at us.

CHAPTER 18

"Get down!" Jackson yelled.

I fell to the bottom of the boat. There was little to conceal us out here. Just the thin wood of the boat.

Jackson jerked the boat to the left, trying to speed away from the other boat. I wished I could tell what was happening, but I didn't dare raise my head for fear a bullet would go through it.

Cold water splashed as the boat swerved. The shock of the cool liquid caused me to draw in a deep breath. But that was the least of my concerns at the moment.

"What are you doing?" I shouted.

"I'm trying to get us back to land."

"You don't want to find out who's shooting at us?"

"I can't."

"Why not?"

"Because there's a hole in my boat."

My eyes widened as I looked down. Sure enough, water was filling the bottom. I'd assumed it had been from the steep turns, but now I saw a small hole near the bottom.

I glanced back. We were still a good five hundred yards from land. Though the water wasn't deep here, it was cold.

I knew all about the dangers of cold water, and I didn't want to think about reliving the moment when I'd nearly lost my life at the hands of a crazy criminal a few weeks back.

Jackson shouted instructions into his phone to someone, one hand still firmly on the steering wheel. The boat moved closer to land. Would we get there in time?

I risked glancing over at the other boat. It sped away. My heart slowed, but only for a moment.

We were safe from flying bullets. But would we go under before we reached dry land?

Water continued to flood the bottom. My shoes were now drenched. The edges of my jeans had absorbed water.

This wasn't good.

It was like the *Titanic* all over again. Only without Leonardo and Kate. And icebergs. And a gigantic, unsinkable cruise ship.

But still.

"We're almost there," Jackson shouted over the roar of the motor.

My first real set of nerves swept over me.

Because someone had just stepped up their game and made it clear that the stakes were deadly.

***

As we waited for the police to arrive, Jackson took me back to his place and led me inside. We hadn't talked all that much on the way here. He'd mostly been on the phone with so many people I'd lost count.

Inside, he led me to the bathroom. It wasn't until we reached the door that he slid his phone into his pocket. His hand grazed my back, making each of my nerves come alive.

"I'll bring you some sweats and a shirt," he said, his voice low and concerned enough to make my muscles feel like jelly. "It should get you through until your clothes dry."

I nodded, so cold that my bones ached. My teeth wouldn't stop chattering, and my fingers were so numb that I hoped I'd be able to unbutton my jeans.

Life seemed determined to kill me with water. Cold water.

I closed the door, locked it—I wasn't even sure why I did that—and put the toilet lid down so I'd have a place to sit. The first thing I did was remove my wet tennis shoes and socks. I could barely feel my feet.

No sooner had I done that did Jackson knock at the door. I unlocked the door and grabbed the clothes he offered. "Thank you."

I quickly stripped out of my clothing and pulled on some black sweatpants and an old 5K T-shirt. The items swallowed me and engulfed me in Jackson's clean scent.

I decided to wear the sweatshirt he'd offered also and quickly pulled it on, hoping it would alleviate my shivers. As soon as I brought it over my head, I pulled the material to my nose and inhaled.

I could drink in this scent all day. It was spicy and clean and masculine.

As soon as I emerged, Jackson thrust some coffee into my hands. To my delight, I saw that he'd added creamer. I'd guess he added sugar also, but I wouldn't know until I took a sip.

"I started a fire," Jackson said. "Why don't you come get warm?"

Before I could argue, he led me there. Ripley already lay in front of the flames. I made myself comfortable on an oversized pillow beside him.

"You're sure you're okay?" Jackson had also changed into some dry jeans and a long-sleeved shirt.

I took a sip of my coffee and nodded. "I'm fine. I promise." I patted a pillow beside me. "Sit for a moment. Warm up before you get sick."

He hesitated before doing just that. The warmth I felt didn't come just from the fire. It also came from somewhere deep inside me, a place where blissful thoughts entertained the idea of cozy romance and undying affection.

"Claire used to love this fireplace," Jackson started.

My heart lurched. He didn't talk about her a lot, but when he did, I took notice.

"What's there not to love?" I said. "Especially if she was here with you, right?"

He nodded soberly. "Yeah."

"So you lived here?" I'd assumed he bought this place more recently.

"We bought this when we moved back to the area. But she was so sick by then, she didn't care about decorating. It was just a place to live. A place to . . ."

He didn't finish. He didn't have to. It had been a place where she'd died.

The thought gripped me, causing a knot in my throat.

Before I could second-guess myself, I reached out. Rested my hand on his cheek.

As soon as I touched him—and electricity darted through me—I realized what I'd done and tried to jerk back. Touching someone's face was level three of personal intimacy in dating. One didn't simply lay their hand on a man's cheek. What had I been thinking?

Before I could withdraw, Jackson's hand covered mine. Our gazes met, and I sucked in a breath.

"Joey, I—"

Before he could finish, someone knocked at the door.

"Jackson, it's Danny!"

The police were here. Of course.

We dropped our hands, but Jackson hesitated for a minute.

"You were going to say?" I started, anticipation sizzling through me.

He propped a knee up, about to stand. "I was going to say: Do you realize that since I've met you, both my truck and boat have been totaled?"

I released my breath. That hadn't been what I'd wanted to hear.

Hashtag: NHPDblueromancestorylinefail.

***

After all the craziness that had happened today,

I'd figured we were done. But as Jackson wrapped up things after the boat shooting, he got another call.

"I've got to get out to Nags Head Woods again," he said after he hung up.

I straightened, still maintaining my place by the fire. "Did you find something about Cora?"

He shook his head. "No, but there's some strange activity going on, and they want the police to come check it out. Ordinarily we'd just send a patrol officer, but since the preserve is tied in with this case, I'm going to check it out myself. I hate to tell you that you have to leave but . . ."

"Then don't. Let me come."

He gave me the *what for* look.

"I won't get in your way. I'll just observe." When he didn't say anything, I decided to try a new tactic. "Mayor Allen would approve. Hashtag: maketheouterbanksgreatagain."

"It's already great."

"Okay, but he wants it to be greater. Or something. I'm not really sure what he's thinking. But as long as he wants me on board, here I am, more than willing to help out."

He sighed. "I have a feeling if I say no, you're just going to show up anyway."

"I would never." I made an expression of

mock offense.

"Mm-hm." He grabbed his keys. "You don't have any time to change. You have to wear that."

I looked down at the oversized sweatpants and sweatshirt. "If you're not ashamed to be seen with me in public."

"Because of your clothes?"

"Ouch. You mean you're ashamed because of who I am?"

"That's not what I meant. I meant I'm not the superficial type, Joey."

Did that mean he wasn't the type to tell me that a makeup artist could do wonders with me? Or that the public would never think I was beautiful if they saw what I really looked like? Jackson had no idea just how much his words meant to me. I wanted someone who liked me for me, not because of what I'd done or what I could do for him.

I cleared my throat. "Then let's go."

Ten minutes later we pulled up to the preserve.

Jackson talked with a woman at the front office who said there had been complaints that people had been in these woods past open hours. Two hikers had seen some suspicious teens in the woods as they left, and she was afraid the high schoolers might deface the property.

That said, Jackson took his flashlight, and we started toward the woods.

I pulled my sweatshirt sleeves down farther over my hands, suddenly wondering if this was a good idea.

But at least I was with Jackson. When I was with him, I knew he wouldn't let anything happen to me.

We stepped off the road onto a narrower trail where the teens had been spotted.

"Any word from your stalker fan club lately?" Jackson asked.

"Not since—" I'd almost said since Elrod got the note from them, but I stopped myself. Jackson didn't know about that, and if he did, he probably wouldn't let me work this case. "No, not recently. Weird, huh?"

"I'd say. But I guess that's good news."

"How about my dad?" I asked, feeling as if a rock settled on my chest. "Any updates on that investigation?"

He shook his head. "I'd let you know if we heard anything. Don't give up hope, Joey. I know it doesn't look like it, but we have several agencies involved in this. We'll find out what happened."

"You mean, you'll find my dad." I didn't miss how he'd worded it. It was almost like he thought he'd find my dad dead. I couldn't believe that. "Not what happened to my dad, like his life was past tense . . ."

"That's not what I meant."

I nodded, the rock pressing harder. "Okay."

"It really wasn't, Joey."

Just then the beam of his flashlight hit something on the side of the path. "Why is there a hole there?" I asked.

Jackson paused and knelt next to it. "Good question."

The hole was probably only six inches in diameter and looked rather crude.

All of Zane's stories about the Goat Man filled my thoughts. Even though I knew the Goat Man wasn't real, I couldn't help but feel uneasy. If Jackson found a small dismembered woodland creature in that hole, I was running back to the visitor center and not looking back.

"It looks fresh," Jackson said.

"So teens are sneaking here to dig holes? Teen vandalism has come a long way since I was in high school. The troublemakers in my town used spray paint to get into trouble."

"It could have been an animal," Jackson said, still studying the dirt. "But based on the edges, I don't think so. I don't see any claw marks."

"Weird."

He stood. "I'll send someone out to look into it tomorrow. For now, let's keep going."

The deeper we went into the woods, the more uncertain I felt about being here. The darkness felt palpable. Animals who called this place home skittered and scattered. The moon was only a sliver, and clouds randomly covered it, reminding me of an enchanted forest.

I hadn't been in the woods at night since . . . since I'd watched the horror movie *The Blair Witch Project*. It had done me in, and I hadn't watched a scary movie since then.

If anything rushed from these trees and grabbed me, I was going to lose something. My courage. My dinner. I couldn't be sure.

"What if we get lost?" I asked Jackson.

"We won't."

"How do you know?" Before he answered, I realized the truth. "You were an Eagle Scout, weren't you?"

He grinned. "How'd you guess?"

"You strike me as the type."

"I'll assume that's a compliment."

Before I could make a witty response that I hadn't come up with yet, the sound of someone running hit my ears. Someone else was in these woods with us. And they didn't want to be seen.

Jackson took off after them, leaving me . . . in

the dark.

CHAPTER 19

I fumbled until I found my phone. Then I fumbled until I found the flashlight feature. And then I fumbled even more as I tried to turn it on. My hands shook too badly. Which was a bummer because I hated the dark and needed to remedy the situation immediately.

Finally, light sliced through the blackness. Yet it wasn't enough. The beam only illuminated a few feet in front of me. I needed more.

Noise in the distance overshadowed my brief line of sight. Jackson shouted. More footsteps pounded. Underbrush snapped and rustled. What was going on?

I paced toward the woods and stopped. I couldn't go off the trail. I'd get lost.

Yet remaining in one place seemed so useless . . . and scary. I gripped my phone more tightly.

Something cracked behind me.

I gasped and twirled around.

My flashlight showed nothing but trees swallowed by gaping black holes.

The Goat Man. He was all I could think of. Stupid Goat Man.

My lungs tightened. I hated this. I should have never agreed to come tonight.

Another twig cracked.

Someone was out there, weren't they? Watching. Waiting.

Who was it? A killer? My stalkers? The person who'd shot at Jackson and me earlier?

I hated this. Had I mentioned that?

The cracks continued, getting closer and closer.

I backed up toward the woods. Away from the sound. From the nighttime intruder.

Or had I intruded into someone else's territory? The thought wasn't comforting.

I took another step, and my ankle hit something. It twisted, and I toppled toward the ground, into the prickly underbrush. Pain raced through my hip, and fear seized me.

I somehow managed to hold on to my phone. With trembling hands, I shone it in the distance.

No one still.

But as my light brushed the ground, it illuminated . . . something.

I squinted. Was that another hole? I sat up and looked closer. Yes, it was.

Why was there another hole out here?

Stupid holes.

"Joey?"

My heart slowed a moment at the familiar voice. "Jackson?"

He stepped into the light, his eyes creasing with concern. "Are you okay?"

I rubbed my arm, feeling silly. "Yeah, I'm fine. Just a little freaked out."

He grabbed my hand and pulled me to my feet. I shook off any imaginary grass and leaves and tried to ignore what was sure to be a big bruise on my hip.

"I guess you didn't catch whoever was out there?" I asked.

"No, he got away. Probably just a teen who was up to no good. Maybe I scared him off, at least."

"Good to know."

He took my arm and led me back in the direction we'd come from. "Come on. I need to get you back. I think we've had enough adventure today."

***

The next day was Sunday. I went to church and sat with Jackson. I'd hoped to have lunch together afterward, but as soon as service was over, Jackson's blind date rushed over and flirted like a woman with no shame.

I almost spared Jackson his misery by feigning already having plans together. But then Elrod texted me. I'd given him my number when he came into Beach Combers. He asked if we could meet right now, and of course I said yes. We arranged to rendezvous at Sunrise Coffee Co. in fifteen.

When I walked inside, I realized my nerves were still shot after being used for target practice yesterday. Despite that, I ordered a soy latte with caramel and an extra pump of chocolate before sitting at a corner table with a great view of the front door. As I waited, I listened to the strands of "Free Fallin'" playing overhead.

The door opened, and Elrod stepped inside. He bypassed ordering anything and marched toward me. At first glance, he seemed a little less defeated and more agitated than the last time I'd seen him.

He tapped his foot nervously as he sat across from me.

I set my drink down. "Elrod, what's going on?"

He leaned toward me, his hands gripping the table, a halfway crazy look in his eyes. "She tried to call me, Joey."

"Who?"

"Cora."

I straightened, certain I hadn't heard him correctly. "What? What do you mean? When?"

He gripped the table even tighter. "She tried to call a couple hours ago, but we got cut off."

My thoughts raced. She was alive. That was the good news. "What did she say?"

"She said, 'Elrod, I need you.'" His voice cracked. "Then I heard someone shout, and the line went dead."

Adrenaline surged through me. Good news with bad news. At least he'd heard from her. "Elrod, did you tell the police? They need to know this. Maybe they can trace the call."

He swung his head back and forth, leaving no room to doubt his choice. "The police think I'm a suspect."

I rested my hand on the table, hoping to reassure him. "I know what that's like. But you have to push past those fears. This could be important. Every minute matters with these things."

He ran a hand over his head and released a long breath. "She wasn't on the phone long enough. I tried to call the number back, and I got nothing. I'm pretty sure it was one of those burner phones."

"You need to let the police figure that out. Elrod, you've got to do it."

"Okay, okay. I can do that. But I can't sleep, Joey. All I can think about is Cora and what she might be going through right now. I can't stand it. She doesn't deserve to suffer."

"She may not be suffering." I hoped my words were true. Prayed they were.

His bloodshot gaze met mine. "You didn't hear her voice, Joey. She sounded terrified."

My concern ricocheted to the next level. I needed more information. Desperately. "Were there any context clues you picked up on? Any noises in the background that might let us know where she might be?"

"No, no . . . I don't think so. I don't know. I was at work. I couldn't hear very well." He blinked and then blinked again, pressing his eyes shut like there was some kind of image he couldn't get out of his mind.

"It's okay. You did the right thing by coming to me." I rocked back and forth in my chair, my thoughts racing. "Elrod, is there any chance she ran away on her own?"

"What? No. Why would you ask that?" His eyes were wide open now and staring at me in shock. "And why would she call me in a state of panic if she did?"

I thought of Lexi again. She'd left for Hollywood on her own and made bad choice after bad choice. Ultimately that led to her death.

"I'm just trying to explore every possibility. It wasn't the photographer. He has an alibi."

"There's got to be someone else!" He slammed his fist onto the table, and my coffee spilled over the edges of the hand-thrown mug.

I glanced over as the barista, Shannon, stared at us, as did another patron. I offered them a reassuring smile. At least, I tried to. "What about some parties Cora started working? Do you know anything about that?"

His face morphed into surprised outrage. "What? What are you talking about? What kind of parties?"

I drew in a deep breath, unsure how he would take this news. There was a good chance he'd cause another scene. "There were some parties hosted by a restaurant owner in this area. He was looking for mermaid impersonators and other exotically themed actresses to attend these shindigs. I believe that Cora may have been paid to go to these gatherings."

"You don't mean—" He stopped, as if he couldn't say the words.

I raised my hand to halt his thoughts. "I don't

think anything like that went down. I think Cora was mostly eye candy for the partygoers."

His face reddened, and his hand fisted and unfisted. "Why didn't she tell me?"

"Maybe because she thought you would react like this." My own pulse raced as I anticipated what he might do next. I prayed he wouldn't turn violent.

He lowered his voice to a hiss. "It's not like that. I would never hurt her."

"I didn't say you would. Was she desperate for money?" I tried to change the subject in an effort to get him to calm down.

He let out a deep breath and ran a hand over his head again. "She wanted to make it big. But she couldn't afford to go to New York or LA. She worked part time at the 99 Center. She could barely pay her bills. So yeah, she wanted money."

"Where did she get the money to pay the photographer?" That question had been bugging me. Andre's services weren't cheap, especially for someone making minimum wage. I wasn't sure how much Billy had paid her, but I'd bet it wasn't five hundred dollars.

"I don't know. I think she cashed out her savings. Maybe she sold something. She didn't tell me. If I asked too many questions, she thought I was being controlling."

I didn't doubt that. "She must have had a lot of hope that this photographer was going to do big things for her."

"She just wanted to be loved. She didn't get it growing up, and I guess I wasn't good enough for her."

Despite my hesitations about the man, compassion swelled in me. "I'm sorry, Elrod. I know this is difficult for you. A lot of actors have a deep-seated need for attention, for various reasons."

I paused, wondering about the truth of those words for my own life. Had I gone into acting to make up for an absent mother who'd chosen modeling over me? I couldn't examine that now, but there was a good chance it was true. I had to shift gears and stay focused on Elrod now.

I leaned closer. "Where did she say she was going last Thursday? Do you remember?"

"Is that when the party was?"

I nodded.

"She said she was going to try and get some extra hours in at the 99 Center. I had no idea that meant she was going to that party."

"Did she act any different after that night?"

He remained in silent thought a moment. "Actually, she did. I didn't think much of it at the time. But she seemed happy. Hopeful. That's when she decided to sign up with that photographer. She said she could feel big things on the horizon."

"So maybe there was a possibility that she did take off. Maybe she didn't want anyone looking for her, so she staged the scene. I know you don't want to consider it, but you should."

"She loved that mermaid tail. She wouldn't run away without it. Besides, she loved me. She wouldn't do this to me." His shoulders drooped. "I know I look guilty. I'll never find her if I'm behind bars."

"Come with me to the police station. The detective is a good man. I promise."

He frowned, and his shoulders slumped even more. "Okay. If you say so."

I walked outside with him and stopped in my tracks on the sidewalk. There was a white truck parked out front . . . just like the one the clerk at 7-Eleven had seen.

CHAPTER 20

I paused and backed up, realizing I could be associating with the bad guy. Without missing a beat, I reached into my purse, grabbed my phone, and hit Jackson's number. Then I set the device aside, hoping Jackson would hear all of this.

Elrod looked back at me, confusion washing over his face. "What?"

I pointed to his truck, my thoughts crashing together. "You followed Cora the day she went missing."

"What? What are you talking about?"

"You've been lying to me, Elrod. And now you're lying again as sure as we stand here in the parking lot of Sunrise Coffee Company." I had to squeeze that in so Jackson would know our location.

Elrod's gangly oversized hands went to his hips as he turned toward me. "Are you losing it? I haven't lied to you."

"The clerk at 7-Eleven saw that white truck at

the convenience store where Cora stopped before her photo shoot. You confronted her in the parking lot and argued." I shielded my eyes from the glare of the sun hitting the truck's windshield.

Elrod let out a long breath, agitation claiming his features. "Stop. Stop! I did follow her, okay?"

"Why?" I took a step back, hoping he didn't lash out. Confronting people was always iffy. Whenever Raven did it, she ended up in hand-to-hand combat, something I clearly wasn't prepared for. "Why would you do that?"

His face pinched, as if he was in pain. "I knew she was up to something. I thought she might be running."

I took another step back and hit the cedar-sided building. "And you wanted to stop her?"

"Yes. No! I mean, it's not like it sounds."

I swallowed hard and moved aside as a thirtysomething couple scooted past us and into the building. "What is it like then, Elrod?"

Elrod paced back and forth. Two steps left. Two steps right. "I thought maybe she'd met someone else."

"Why would you think that?" *Please, Jackson. Be listening. Be on your way!*

"Because of that spring in her step. I didn't put it there. She'd supposedly been at work the night before. But I stopped by. She wasn't there."

So he hadn't been telling me the truth earlier. I didn't like that. "Did you ask her about it?"

Elrod's gaze darkened. "She said she went to see a friend instead. That's all she would tell me. I know her friends. She wasn't with them."

"So you assumed she was cheating on you."

"It was a logical assumption. I needed to know."

He was definitely possessive. That didn't usually lead to good things. "What were you going to do if Cora was cheating on you?"

His eyes widened, as if he realized the implications of what he'd said. "I wasn't going to hurt her, if that's what you're getting at. I needed to know. I needed to move on. No one strings along Elrod. No one!"

Talking about oneself in third person was never a good sign . . . *right, Joey?* "So you talked to her outside of 7-Eleven and tried to get some of the answers she owed you."

"I did. I borrowed my friend's truck."

"No wonder the police didn't connect the dots."

"My own truck isn't working right now. I'm trying to save money to have it fixed."

"Yet your girlfriend came gallivanting out here with all that money while you were working hard. That might cause some resentment."

"You're trying to trap me." His voice trembled as he stared at me, his eyes full of accusation. "I thought you were different."

"I'm not trying to trap you, Elrod. I'm trying to get the truth. You're doing all kinds of dances around it."

He paced back to his truck and leaned against it. He looked both guilty and burdened as he squeezed the skin between his eyes. "I followed her. I just wanted to know if she was cheating. We've been dating a long time, and I've never seen her look like that. Or not tell me something. Why wouldn't she tell me what was going on? Unless she'd met someone else." He swung his head back and forth, sobering even more. "I've always known Cora was out of my league."

I glanced in my purse and saw my screen was still lit. I just needed to keep Elrod talking until the police got here. "What did she say when you confronted her?"

"She said she was pursuing an opportunity that could be good for both of us. I asked her to tell me what, and she said she couldn't."

"Did you ask why?"

"Of course. She said it was dangerous."

"Dangerous?" I hadn't expected him to say that. "Why?"

"She wouldn't say. She just said she had to do something, and as soon as she could, she'd tell me what it was. Until then she had to do things her way."

"What about the umbrella stand?"

"What?" He looked at me, dumbfounded from his parted lips to his blank stare.

"She bought an umbrella stand inside 7-Eleven. Why would she do that? How did that tie in with this dangerous opportunity she was pursuing?"

"I have no idea. Maybe she was going to start selling umbrellas?"

I shook my head. "No, that's lame."

"You asked."

"Something happened at that party. Some opportunity. Find that out and maybe we'll find Cora." I was challenging myself, not Elrod.

Just then Jackson pulled up. Jackson. Good. He could take over now.

***

I sat on a bright-blue bench outside of Sunrise Coffee Co., trying to stay out of the way. Shannon—the barista—had been a saint and brought me another latte. I'd asked her to bring black coffee for Jackson as well.

I watched—quietly, had I said that yet?—as another officer put Elrod in the back of a police cruiser. He would go in for questioning, and the police would get to the bottom of both Cora's phone call and Elrod's half-truths.

As they pulled away, Jackson turned toward me, and I waited for his praise and commendation.

I blinked up at him, my most winning smile on my face. "Aren't you proud of me? I called you first."

His gaze remained humorless. Had I interrupted him from another date with Ms. Blonde and Perky? Because I thought he'd look happy.

"How did you know Elrod?" he asked.

"What do you mean, 'how did you know Elrod'?" Had I given yet something else away? Probably. An uncomfortable feeling clenched my gut.

"You were meeting with him."

"Okay . . ." He was getting at something, but I wasn't sure what.

"Rachel may have said his first name, but she didn't offer enough information for this meeting to happen on its own."

I shrugged as reality hit me. I'd been caught. Again. "I don't know what you want me to say."

Shannon—the barista—interrupted us by bringing Jackson that coffee I'd requested. He only looked 50 percent grateful though. Never a good sign. His gaze was smoldering on mine, and I knew he wasn't going to let this drop.

"Do you have a little side investigation going on, Joey?" he asked.

My throat tightened so quickly I could hardly breathe. "What do you mean?"

"I mean that could be a conflict of interest. If you're doing side jobs, you can't be working with the police."

"But—"

He stepped back, that no-nonsense look still on his face. "Think about it, Joey."

His words cooled me. He was angry. I'd known he would be if he'd found out Elrod had approached me for help. But I'd just turned the man in. How could Jackson still be upset?

Jackson left, and I was fuming when I climbed back into my car. I couldn't go back to my place. I obviously wasn't going to be invited to the police station to watch Elrod be questioned.

So I did the next best thing. I decided to drive to Moyock. I wanted to talk to Rachel. Maybe stop by the 99 Center, where she and Cora had worked together. Do anything to find answers. Do anything to get rid of guilt.

As the beach landscape turned into farmland, I reflected on what I knew.

I knew that Cora Day desperately wanted to be famous. She'd somehow scrounged up five hundred dollars for pictures from a supposed world-famous photographer with connections. Andre's alibi after that photo session seemed to hold up, and he was the last one seen with Cora.

She'd bought an umbrella stand for some reason.

She'd attended that party Billy hosted and had left early, looking upset.

I sighed. I felt like I'd done a lot of work, but nothing seemed to get me closer to any answers.

My phone rang. Rutherford's name popped onto the screen. Go figure.

With a less than enthusiastic hello, I answered.

"The beach life not as sunny as you'd hoped it would be?" Rutherford asked.

I didn't tell him my response was based on my lack of desire to go back to Hollywood right now. I had only a few days until I left, and I wasn't sure I was ready to face my old life. "I didn't say that."

"Well, I've got some good news," Rutherford said. "Netflix is interested in picking up *Relentless*."

My spine went stiff as I stared at the road ahead. "What?"

"It's true. They're in talks now."

"What?" I repeated, still not sure if I'd heard correctly. Of all the things I'd expected to hear, that was not one of them.

"Joey, your TV series might be resurrected from the dead. That's what they did with *Longmire*, *Full House*, and *Gilmore Girls*. I thought you'd be happy."

My heart twisted, a mix of excitement and hesitation. *Relentless* had been canceled after some disputes on the set. And I'd come here to find my dad, which I hadn't done yet. I couldn't leave until I did.

But I needed to face the possibility that I might not ever find him. What would I do then? Remain here for decades without answers? I couldn't support myself on this salary forever.

"Joey?" Rutherford said.

I gripped the steering wheel tighter. "I don't know what to say."

"Well, nothing is definite yet. I just thought I'd let you know. For now, you just worry about *Family Secrets*. You do have your plane tickets and a dress for the premiere, right?"

"Of course."

"Great. You're in for some ride, Joey. I know

you think your career is dead, but I think it's just starting. Hold on for the ride."

I hung up and leaned back against my seat.

Was that what I wanted? To resurrect my career? To be adored by millions? To have my face on magazine covers? People would give up everything to be in my shoes.

But I didn't see the decision as easy as that.

And I had no idea what I'd do if Netflix offered me a contract. It didn't matter right now. Because I was in Moyock. Now I needed to find Rachel and have a long chat. I'd deal with one problem at a time.

CHAPTER 21

I pulled up to the 99 Center, a square, lonely building on a long stretch of country highway. I hoped I might catch Rachel here.

I stepped inside, and sickly sweet elevator music assaulted my ears. Every aisle and walkway in front of me was crammed with cheap trinkets, deceptively portioned bargain snacks, and anemic-looking stuffed animals. It was like the prize counter at Chuck E. Cheese's, only in grown-up store form.

To my delight and amazement, Rachel was behind the counter. She wore a money-green polo, still sported poorly applied makeup, and had two pigtail braids. She looked bored as she studied her hair for split ends. Thankfully, it wasn't busy inside.

Rachel's eyes lit up when she spotted me. "Joey Darling? I can't believe you're here."

I approached the register and rested my hands on the counter in an unassuming pose.

Body Language 101. "I had a few questions, and I thought this might be the easiest way to talk."

She stiffened. "Is that right? Did you find Cora? Is there an update?"

"No, there's not, unfortunately. But everyone's working hard to figure out what happened to her."

She nibbled on her bottom lip. "I've been so worried about her. At first I wondered if she'd just pulled another stunt and taken off. But it's been six days, and no one has heard from her."

I considered mentioning the fact that Elrod had heard from her, but I decided not to. There was no need to get her worked up.

"I was watching this *48 Hours*–type of show, and a girl on there disappeared. They found her body a year later. It's been all I could think about since then. What if that's Cora's story too?" Rachel's voice cracked, and she ran a finger under her eye where moisture had formed.

Compassion pressed on me. "That's not going to be Cora's story. You've got to stay positive. But could you answer a few questions for me? There are some things that don't make sense."

"I'll do anything. Ask away."

I jammed my hip against the counter. "Why would Cora say she was coming into some money?"

The color drained from Rachel's face. "I . . . I don't know."

I highly doubted that. "Rachel . . . I know you want to help. You've got to tell me the truth."

Rachel began to straighten a rack of mints, her fingers trembling uncontrollably. "I pinky promised I wouldn't tell anyone."

"Cora's life could be in danger."

She shoved a box of Tic Tacs in the display a little too hard, and all the candies fell from the rack. I helped her pick them up and gave her time to gather her thoughts.

"She quit her job here," Rachel blurted, her hands flailing in the air, the Tic Tacs forgotten.

I blanched. "What?"

"It's true. Last Friday was her final day. It was all very sudden."

"How did she plan on paying her bills without a job?"

"That's what I wanted to know. But she had this new light in her eyes, and she said everything was going to work out."

"Why was that a secret? You said she told you not to talk about it."

Rachel leaned closer, even though there was no one else within eyesight or earshot. "She said it was all hush-hush, and if I talked about it, I could ruin everything. It didn't make sense to me, but what did I know?"

This was growing more interesting by the minute. "Did she tell Elrod?"

"No, she thought Elrod overreacted too much. She said she was only going to tell me and no one else."

That was just one more reason to suspect Elrod. She was keeping a lot of secrets from him. "She was at a party last Thursday, wasn't she?"

Rachel nodded, her face a ghostly white that clearly showed she was thinking the worst.

"So she could have found out something there," I murmured aloud, trying to work through my thoughts. "Maybe someone offered her a job."

Rachel ran the end of the braid against her cheek and sighed. "I don't think so. She was finally going to be able to follow her dreams. That's when she lined up the photo session. She could barely make her rent. I have no idea how she expected to pay that expensive photographer."

"Maybe she used the money Billy paid her."

"He only paid a hundred bucks for the gig."

I shifted, still trying to shift through what I knew. "Did she say anything else about these parties? Something that might indicate where she thought she'd get this money?"

"She just said that her presence there was serendipitous. That was her exact word."

Two puzzle pieces suddenly clicked in my head. "Did you say she developed her unusual interest in Nags Head Woods before or after the party?"

"After. We went there the day she quit work here."

That was the connection, I realized. But why? What about Nags Head Woods might have made her come into a windfall?

Someone who'd been at that party knew, I realized. And I needed to find out who.

***

Thankfully, Phoebe texted me and reminded me that we were supposed to meet tonight at Meatsa Eatsa, a local burger joint that ground their own beef every single day and made it into the most delicious patties one would ever taste.

For real. Just thinking about those burgers expanded my waist by two inches.

Phoebe was waiting in a booth when I walked in. The scent of grease and grilled beef filled the air. I hated to admit it, but I loved those scents. Especially when they were together.

Girlfriend time seemed like such a foreign

concept to me. I'd always seemed to connect better with guys, ever since grade school. That said, I didn't think that was the healthiest thing for me. Every woman needed a girlfriend in her life.

Phoebe waved me over, and I slid in across from her.

I would not order a yummy hamburger tonight. No, I'd get a salad. Because I was dedicated to complete healthy eating like that.

But when the waitress came, I totally found myself ordering a burger. With cheese. And bacon.

Do you know what that meant? It meant I wouldn't fit into the dress I'd gotten for my movie premiere. And I'd look bloated on *Good Morning America*. But it was too late to change my order. That was what I told myself, at least.

I was in trouble.

But I still didn't flag the waitress down.

"What's going on?" Phoebe asked, taking a sip of her soda. "You seemed frazzled."

"You say that a lot. In nearly every conversation, for that matter."

She shrugged, looking halfway apologetic. "Let's say you're not one to wander into town and relax. You seem to have a 'seek out and destroy' radar for trouble in the area."

"That's one way to say it. Is it my fault that everyone just assumes I'll be an awesome detective like Raven? Or that those who don't, want to keep Raven alive by manipulating me into getting involved in troubling situations?"

"It's an interesting life you lead. I think I'll keep my boring one though."

Before I could respond with something witty—something I hadn't come up with yet—a guy approached the table. My shoulders tightened. Someone else asking for my autograph? Perhaps. But when I looked up to offer my most winning smile, I noticed he wasn't looking at me at all. He was looking at Phoebe.

"How's it going, Pheebs?"

She smiled warmly in return. "Robbie. It's going. I didn't expect to see you here. This is my friend, Joey."

"Nice to meet you." His gaze only stayed on me a minute before locking on Phoebe again. "I was wondering when I'd run into you again."

Phoebe shoved a stray hair behind her ear, not looking quite as laid back as she normally did. "I've been around. It sounds like you've been busy. That's what Tony said the last time I ran into him."

"I've been doing tile work on some new houses in Duck," he said. "It's a paycheck, but I don't dig the drive. I'm on the road from Hatteras for at least an hour." He shrugged. "Anyway, I swung by here on my way home. Don't feel like cooking by the time I get back to my place."

"I get that."

He fidgeted, his gaze not leaving Phoebe. "I can't wait until it's warm again so we can hit the waves."

"It will be awesome." Phoebe's cheeks reddened slightly.

Oh my goodness. Phoebe liked this guy. I quickly soaked him in. He was probably our age. He wore a backward baseball cap, baggy jeans, and a well-worn surf shirt. Typical attire for this area. He had a boyish cuteness about him, almost like he was bashful, which was just adorable.

"Well, it was good seeing you."

He nodded to me before stepping away. When he was out of earshot, I turned to Phoebe. "Oh my goodness! He totally likes you."

"No, he doesn't." She blushed. Blushed!

"Oh, he does. Who is he?"

"He's just a guy I know." She clearly didn't want to say more.

"He's cute."

"It's complicated," she said.

I nodded. "I get complicated. I really do."

She readjusted her weight against the padded

bench as the waitress delivered our food. "So, not to change the subject, but I'm going to totally change the subject. Are you going to stick around in this area for long?"

I drew in a deep breath, the question surprising me. "That is a great question. This was only meant to be a layover until I could figure things out."

"And then it's back to Hollywood?"

I shrugged and stared at my glass of water. "I don't know. I don't really want to return there. And I do. I'm torn between living a life that could be exceptional and living a life that could be ordinary."

"Is there anything wrong with ordinary?"

"No, exceptional is pretty overrated." I attempted a smile but failed.

"Well, I know one thing. You're going to have some broken hearts if you decide to leave."

My breath caught at her unexpected revelation. "I am? Who?"

She let her head drop to the side in a "duh" expression. "Do I really have to tell you that?"

"My man radar needs some serious readjusting." I wasn't sure I'd ever trust it again after Eric.

"I see. I'll let you figure it out. I'd just hate to see good people get hurt, Joey."

What I'd hoped might be a lighthearted evening suddenly felt heavy. Very heavy. But I couldn't fault Phoebe for her words. She was right. I needed to think about the consequences of my actions. I refused to leave a path of destruction behind me anymore.

In the meantime, I needed to eat this burger before it got cold.

CHAPTER 22

Golfing.

I remembered hearing Siegfried, as he'd slipped into a conversation with another man about how much he loved to golf, say that he would meet someone on the greens on Monday at four.

And since I had no other ideas on how to track down people from the party, I decided to look at the area's golf courses. Thankfully, aside from mini-golf, there weren't that many places to hit the green here in the Outer Banks. I decided to start with the most logical location: a course in Nags Head.

After work and with the sun sinking on the horizon, I pulled up to the golf course. Just as I parked and walked toward the club building, I spotted someone familiar walking out with a golf bag slung over his shoulder.

Jackpot! It was Ryan, Siegfried's geeky brother.

His steps slowed when he saw me. "I met you at that party, didn't I?"

I nodded, feeling like I should have some golf equipment with me to sell my cover story. But I didn't, so I hoped I might be able to rent some inside, if it came down to it.

"You sure did," I said. "I didn't realize you played golf. I'm just here to play a few . . ." What were they called? My mind went blank. "Innings. Quarters, I mean."

"Rounds?" He raised his eyebrows, still looking like he didn't trust me.

"Exactly. That's what I said. Rounds."

He didn't appear convinced. "Siegfried likes coming here. It helps him unwind."

"I see. And you're always there for your brother, it sounds like."

"This is his territory. I'm only here temporarily." He pushed his glasses up higher.

"How long is your vacation?"

He shrugged. "I actually got laid off from my job with a tech company. I decided to enjoy the time off until I can find a new job."

"It's good to take some time to reflect. What else have you done in this area? Anything besides golf? Because there are so many good options. Jockey's Ridge, the National Seashore, Nags Head Woods, just to name a few."

I watched his expression to see if he'd show any signs of recognition. He remained stoic. "We're not here for fun. Not really. Mostly a rest between work. We've golfed and done some shooting at the range."

My throat tightened when I remembered the gunfire on Jackson's boat. "Shooting?"

He nodded. "My brother is a skilled marksman. Really, anything he tries his hand at, he succeeds in."

That was very good to know. "A marksman, huh?"

"That's right. My dad used to come to this area all the time to hunt. It must run in the family. But not me. I prefer computers and coding."

"I never did understand exactly what business you and your brother were in."

Before he could answer, I heard a footstep behind me. "If it isn't the hottie from Billy's party!"

I turned and saw Siegfried in all his smug fakeness standing there.

"Small world," I muttered.

"I was hoping I might see you again." He stared me up and down like I was an Armani suit and he had the urge to dress to impress.

"Were you?" I repeated, unsure what else to

say. I didn't want to flirt back and reward his bad behavior. I *could* do it. I *could* utilize my acting skills and make this work. But I wouldn't. Not right now.

"I was kicking myself after the party."

"Why's that?" My voice sounded tight as I asked the question.

His eyes twinkled with arrogance. "Because I wanted to ask you out."

I blinked, trying to keep my expression neutral and not show my disdain. "Did you?"

"That's right. So what do you say?"

That'd I'd rather go on Dancing with the Stars. Instead I said, "You're serious?"

"Of course I'm serious. Tonight." He glanced at his watch. "In two hours. Is that enough time?"

I had no desire to eat with this man. However, this could be my opportunity to find out more information. Could I really pass it up? Of course not. "Can I pick the place?"

"Name it."

"It won't be Willie Wahoo's."

"Good. That place is a dump." He offered a guttural half chuckle, half groan of disgust.

"Okay then. Let's do it. Fatty Shack in two hours." I turned to leave.

"I thought you came to play golf," Ryan called.

Oh yeah . . . "I was, but now I've got to get

ready for a date. Golf will have to take a time-out."

***

I briefly thought about telling Jackson about my date with Siegfried. But that just felt so high maintenance. And I'd picked a location that was very public. And I wouldn't do anything stupid like go somewhere alone with Siegfried.

So I should be fine.

Said every woman before she ended up dead because of a stupid choice.

While still in my car outside the restaurant, I ran a hand through my hair and tried to remain calm. I liked to think that I knew what I was doing, when in truth, I had no idea what I was doing. Except trying to find some answers. And trying to stay alive, and trying to get some kind of justice in a world that seemed so unjust sometimes. Justice for Cora. Justice for Lexi.

I played with my hair. I'd taken the time to add some soft waves, and I wore it down over my shoulders. I'd picked my favorite jeans and a nice black top to go with them. And heels. Always heels on dates.

I wasn't trying to impress, but I'd decided to play a role since it was what I did best. Tonight

I'd tap into the sophisticated actress side of me. And I'd do it all for the sake of gaining information.

I stepped into Fatty's, a quaint little restaurant located on the causeway between Nags Head and Roanoke Island. It was run by locals who used fresh local seafood and vegetables whenever possible. The place wasn't beautiful, and it usually smelled like both grease and disinfectant, but the food and atmosphere were otherwise good.

I'd come here before both with Zane and with Jackson. I'd do anything to be with either of them now instead of Siegfried. But that wasn't an option. Instead, I would suffer this out with Shania Twain, who crooned overhead.

My eyes scanned the eating area and came to a stop on Siegfried. My stomach roiled at the sight of him. Based on his still-wet hair, he was freshly showered. His fake tan had been sprayed. His extra-white teeth glistened.

He was trouble. I felt sure about it.

I plastered on a smile and sauntered over to him. He rose when he saw me.

"Joey," he said.

I nodded and lowered myself gracefully into my seat. I could be graceful when I was pretending to be someone I wasn't.

I should totally get points for that.

"I went ahead and ordered some calamari." He nodded toward the basket at the center of the table.

I glanced at the golden, greasy fried squid and tried not to turn up my nose. "Looks great."

I really wanted to jump right to the point. I wanted to ask questions about Cora. But if I did, he'd run from me. If he'd been the man who was shooting at me, then he might do worse than run. He might start shooting again. That was why I had to play this cool.

No sooner had the thought popped into my mind, did a gaggle of commotion clamor near the restaurant's entrance. I closed my eyes, instantly knowing who else was here tonight.

The Hot Chicks.

"Joey! I had no idea you were going to be here!" Dizzy cackled. "And who is this?"

I bit back my dread. This wasn't supposed to happen. "This is Siegfried."

Siegfried looked unabashedly annoyed as the group surrounded our table. "Hello."

Dizzy's mouth opened in an exaggerated *O*. "You're always so full of surprises, Joey. Well, we'll let you two eat. Enjoy!"

However, it was going to be hard to enjoy, I realized, as the group sat behind me. All I could hear was their opinions on man buns—unfortunately, they hadn't grasped the meaning of that yet and were talking about a different kind of man buns. Then they talked about the Romeos again. They were worse than a group of high school girls.

I swallowed and tried to concentrate on Siegfried.

Thankfully, the waitress came and took our order. Siegfried got a steamer basket, and I ordered shrimp scampi on a bed of broccoli instead of noodles.

Winning!

"So tell me about yourself," I started, raising my water glass. "What do you do for a living? I don't think you've told me yet."

"I'm a professor."

My eyebrows shot up. I hadn't expected that one.

"I get that reaction a lot." He smiled, as if satisfied.

I kept my voice smooth and flirty as I said, "You don't strike me as the professor type."

"Because I'm not wearing elbow patches and a sweater vest?"

"Perhaps. None of my professors looked like you." I puked in my mouth a little as I said the words.

He cocked his head. "I had no idea you went to college."

Ouch! I leaned back to observe him better and keep my emotions in check. "Was that an insult?"

"That was whatever you want, I suppose." His eyes twinkled.

I wanted to smack that sparkle from his gaze, the big old jerk. I did not like this man. Not one little bit.

"If you're a professor, what are you doing in this area? Do you teach at one of the colleges? Are there any colleges on the Outer Banks even?" I tried to think it through, but I couldn't remember what was here.

He straightened the crisp sleeves of his shirt. "I'm writing a book, if you must know. This area is fascinating, and I'm researching its history."

I nodded, like I was interested. "It really is. Pirates. Shipwrecks. Submarines off the coast during World War II."

"You know more than I thought."

Was that another dig at my intelligence? I didn't want to think so. But maybe I should. I stabbed my lemon with my straw, wishing I had something stronger than water.

"Where do you teach?"

"All over."

"And what do you teach?" Sheesh. Most men loved to talk about themselves. Siegfried was a little too calculating for that though. He wanted me to work for answers. It was one more way of being controlling.

"History."

Before I could continue my questions, Erma—our waitress—delivered our food in record time. I had to keep the conversation going before the subject changed.

I raised a fork but didn't dig into the tantalizing food on the table. Not yet. I saw my opening. "Fascinating. You know where I went for the first time the other day? Nags Head Woods."

His eyes lit, but only for a moment. "Is that right?"

I nodded. "I was looking for the Goat Man."

The tension seemed to leave him, and he let out a long chuckle. "The Goat Man. The idea is utterly ridiculous."

"But is it?"

"The woods are much more fascinating than that. There used to be an entire village there. Sea captains made it their home. The land tells the tale of a long history fraught with hardship and survival."

"It sounds like it. I can't imagine the ways

they had to contend with Mother Nature. It's rough, even with all our modern technologies. But back then they had none of that."

"No, they used their instincts—something we've lost in our lazy culture."

"Fascinating."

"Now on the other hand, the time period truly was fascinating. I can only imagine what it was like back then. Pirates. A disappearing colony of people. Contending with Native Americans. It was an adventure."

"And that's what your book touches on?"

"That and more."

I forced a smile. "How are you doing research?"

"Various ways. Estate sales. Some of the houses here were built with scraps from shipwrecks. One man in Hatteras found a trunk up in his attic with journals inside. He's been letting me read them. Relatives of the Mullits were mentioned in it."

"The Mullits?"

"The cemeteries at Nags Head Woods? They're filled with Mullits."

"So they're journals of a sea captain and his family?"

"That's right. It paints a different picture of what life was like on this island, back before people first started coming here because they thought the ocean promoted health, healing, and longevity."

"I see. It certainly sounds like you're going to have one great book at the end of this process." I shifted and stabbed a piece of shrimp. This was all interesting, but I wanted to know about Cora. "I'm still trying to figure out how an esteemed historian like yourself got mixed up with Billy."

"I could ask the same thing about you."

"True. How many parties have you been to?"

He cooled in front of me. "Are you interrogating me?"

"Can't a girl just make conversation?" And I wasn't ready to let this drop yet. "What's up with the mermaids there? And the Egyptian princesses."

He shrugged, my explanation seeming to appease him. "Beats me. Billy likes them. I think he really wants to live in Vegas, but since he doesn't, he's bringing Vegas here."

"I see." I leaned closer. "The truth is, I got connected with Billy's parties through a friend." I held up the picture on my phone. "Maybe you recognize her?"

He stared at Cora's photo, and his face went pale.

CHAPTER 23

"Why would you ask that?" Siegfried's gaze darkened.

I laced my fingers together and posed with them below my chin. I was the picture of innocence, especially when I added in some fluttered eyelashes. "Can't a girl just be curious?"

His eyes further darkened into bottomless abysses. "I'm not buying it."

Sell your acting skills, Joey. This is what you do. And remember: the best lies are grounded in the truth.

"Look, all I'm saying is my friend went to Billy's parties. I just wondered if you'd ever seen her. Based on your reaction, I'd say yes. Also based on your reaction, something about Cora bothers you. Otherwise, you wouldn't hem and haw."

"Hem and haw?" He chortled. "Now that's a backwoods expression."

Oh, I'll show you backwoods.

I was close to answers. I could feel it in my bones, and I couldn't blow it now.

"Yeah, I remember seeing her there." He pushed his food away, as if he'd lost this appetite.

I squinted. "What aren't you saying, Siegfried?"

"There's nothing I'm not saying."

He was definitely defensive.

"You know Cora is missing, don't you?" I let out a dramatic gasp. "Are you acting like this because you had something to do with her disappearance?"

His hands hit the table. "What? No. Is this the reason you wanted to meet me? Because if it is, I'm done."

I knew there was no recovering from this now. I had to charge full speed ahead.

"I'm going to have to report this to the police, you know."

"There's nothing to report." His voice rose until everyone quieted around us. "I didn't do anything to that girl. I haven't seen her since that night."

I wanted to lean toward him in interrogation mode, but I needed to keep things as light as possible. "Then why the overreaction?"

He wiped a hand over his face and glanced around. He lowered his voice. "I hit on her, alright? She wasn't interested. But I made a move. I was rejected."

"Is that right?" I was certain he didn't take well to that.

"She acted interested, but she wasn't. Are you happy now?" His shoulders sagged as his false pride dissipated like fog on a sunny day.

"I don't know if I'm happy, but at least I'm partly satisfied."

He shifted and sighed, as if this conversation was beneath him. "Listen, when did she disappear?"

"Sunday."

"I was doing a lecture on Sunday. All day. In Raleigh. Ask anyone."

"Good to know."

"That said, I can tell you're not here because you're interested in me—"

Like I'm the superficial one here.

"—and I'm done." He threw his napkin on the table. "Have a great life, Joey Darling. You don't know what you're missing out on."

Oh, but I did. And I was so glad to be missing out on any type of future with a narcissist.

He stormed from the restaurant, but I wasn't in a hurry to go anywhere. I used my phone to do an Internet search for Siegfried. I did a quick check to confirm if he'd spoken at the college in Raleigh. Sure enough, there were announcements and even a couple of Twitter feeds about the event.

"That didn't go well, huh?" Dizzy called from behind me.

"No, it didn't. But I'm getting closer to the truth."

Since Siegfried didn't leave any money, I dropped some hard-earned cash on the table. Then it was time for me to go.

I needed to think things through a little more.

Five minutes later, I pulled up to my oceanfront duplex.

When I stepped out of my car, someone else stepped out of the shadows.

Billy. And he held a baseball bat.

CHAPTER 24

"I thought I told you to stay out of this." Billy patted a bat in his hands. He looked menacing, pure and simple.

I gripped my keys, shoving them between my fingers like a domestic housewife version of Wolverine. I could turn these suckers into weapons. If I needed to, I could use my baloney move. I was not going to act like a scared little fawn ducking into the woods. Besides, there were no woods to duck into.

That said, I really hoped Zane might step out or Jackson might drive past.

"What are you doing here, Billy?" I asked.

He narrowed his eyes, still gripping that stick. "I know you were with Siegfried tonight."

I raised my chin. "Are you dictating who I can go on dates with now?"

He stepped closer. "You and I both know that was no date."

"You're being awfully presumptuous." My

backwoods-mountain attitude tried to claw its way out of me again, but I attempted to hold it at bay. "What you think doesn't mean diddly squat, and you have no idea who my type is."

Umph! There it was. My backwoods dialect had come out after all, and all signs of the sophisticated Joey disappeared.

He glared at me. "No, but I can guess."

"I think you're a jerk." Oops. Where had that come from? I flinched.

"You need to back off," Billy growled.

"You view me as a threat." I raised my chin higher, knowing my words were true.

My declaration obviously threw him off guard because he froze a moment before chuckling. "You're a menace. Like a mouse or a mosquito. But you're no threat."

I jutted a hip out. "Have we forgotten about the Zika virus?"

Again, my words seemed to throw him. He blinked, as if I were a loon. He didn't know what to do with me, and I needed to use that to my advantage.

"I don't know what you're up to, but I'll figure it out," I said, gripping my keys more tightly.

He smirked. "Another overt threat, Joey? Didn't you learn last time? This is your last warning," he growled. "Don't make me sic my guys on you."

His words caused a tremble to rake through me.

Just then the door opened, and Zane stepped out with a glass of green juice in his hands.

"Joey? Everything okay?" He squinted. "Billy?"

Billy waved, suddenly looking chummy and his bat looking more like a baton as he twirled it between his fingers. "I was just leaving."

I waited until he was gone—he'd parked his car in the driveway next door, and I hadn't spotted it when I pulled in. Once he'd pulled away, I joined Zane by the door.

"What was that about?" Zane asked.

"He thinks I'm getting too close to the answers, and he warned me to back off."

Zane frowned. "I don't like bullies, Joey. Maybe you *should* back off."

I shook my head. "Do you know what I do when people try to pressure me? It gives me incentive to keep pushing back. And that's what I intend to do."

***

In the privacy of my duplex, I curled up on the couch with my grandmother's quilt comforting me. I needed some quiet time to think this through. Actually, I'd welcome thinking it through with someone else as a sounding board, but Zane had gotten a phone call from his family and left early to take the call. They lived in Florida now, from what I understood, and his dad was having some heart problems.

Okay, Joey, let's review your suspects. Starting with Siegfried.

Even though the man might be sleazy, he didn't appear to be guilty.

Elrod apparently was innocent.

How about Billy? Could he have been upset with Cora and taken revenge? He didn't seem like the type to abduct. He'd just kill someone and walk away.

Andre supposedly had an alibi as well.

Whom did that even leave?

Maybe I needed to review each of my previous suspects a little more closely. Verify alibis. Look for cracks. Examine the three Rs: a reason, a resource, and a right circumstance.

Jackson was right—I seemed to care about this case to the extreme. I had so much guilt in my past. If I could help Cora, maybe just a little bit of the burden I carried could be lifted. It would be a start in making things right.

With a sigh, I picked up my dad's old Bible. I'd

found it in a storage shed where he'd left some of his most prized possessions before he disappeared, and I now kept it on my end table. When I felt blue, I picked it up. Right now, as memories washed over me, I rubbed the leather cover.

My dad had used this Bible. A lot. I wondered if he'd pored over the words of comfort found here after my mom abandoned us. I wondered if he'd felt those same emotions—that same sense of abandonment—when I'd left for Hollywood. When I'd told him I never wanted to see him again.

That couldn't be our last conversation. It just couldn't.

Tears pushed to my eyes.

I opened the well-used book and saw my dad's handwriting scrawled on the edges of the pages. He'd taken notes and underlined his favorite verses. He was such a man of faith. He'd chased God. You know whom I'd chased? Myself. That needed to change.

Sure, in some ways I was looking out for Cora by doing this investigation. But I couldn't sustain this lifestyle of being a wannabe investigator forever. None of it was meant to be permanent. None of it was supposed to happen at all, for that matter.

But now I'd been roped into not only this mystery but the mystery of my father's disappearance. On top of those things, my mother had reappeared in a photo I'd found belonging to my dad. Was she somehow involved in all of this? After all, her modeling career had never taken off. What had she done?

When I'd been a teenager, I'd Googled her a few times, but nothing had ever come up. It was almost like she'd been wiped off the face of the earth.

Nothing made sense.

I glanced down and saw one verse in particular was highlighted. Isaiah 40:31. *But those who hope in the Lord will renew their strength. They will soar on wings like eagles; they will run and not grow weary, they will walk and not be faint.*

I closed my eyes. Was my dad sending me a message, even though he was nowhere near? Because those words were just what I needed to hear.

I needed to keep on pressing forward, no matter how much of a failure I felt like.

CHAPTER 25

I did some haircuts the next morning. When I was done, I made a trip to Manteo as a part of my Operation Requestion the Supposedly Innocent.

I was starting with Andre. I'd overheard Jackson talking, and I knew this was where the faux photographer lived. He'd made it sound like he came down from New York, but he hadn't. He'd moved here a few months ago from Arkansas, probably to find a new group of people to prey on. I'd also found out that his name really wasn't Andre Delacroix but Andrew Delaware. Some people.

And I had questions for him.

I marched right up to his little white bungalow, located on a decent piece of property on the outskirts of Manteo. I wondered if he'd paid for this place with money from his scams. What he was doing was despicable.

Andre answered the door with a camera draped across his bare chest. I heard a female in the background, and I didn't even try to hide my eye roll.

His smile quickly disappeared when he recognized me. He tried to shut the door, but my hand jetted out and blocked him. It was a Raven move, and I didn't know I had it in me.

"We need to talk," I said.

His hand remained on the door, and he kept pushing. I kept pushing back. If he was innocent, why was he so defensive?

"Is that necessary?" he whispered. "Didn't we already talk? Maybe I could show you some of the photos I took of you instead?"

"You already sold those to the *Instigator*, didn't you?"

His cheeks reddened, and I knew I'd hit on the truth. Apparently, even though he'd dropped the device into the water, either he'd been able to salvage the SD card, or he'd used technology that had instantly transferred his pictures to a server of some sort.

"I could sue you for invasion of privacy," I told him. I didn't know if that was the truth or not, but I'd bet Andre didn't know either.

He raised his hands. "I'm just a guy trying to make some extra cash. You can't fault me for that."

"Sure I can, especially when you try to make cash by exploiting others. That's what you thrive on."

"It's not like that."

"Andre, is everything okay?" a female said in the distance.

I glanced beyond him and saw a woman in a bikini standing at the back of the house. I'd bet my two eye teeth she was another client in the middle of a photo shoot.

"*Oui, oui, ma cherie!*" Andre said, slipping back into French mode.

"He's not French," I called over his shoulder.

Andre ran a hand over his face before giving me a dirty look. "Must you?"

"Baby?" She stepped closer, a pouty expression on her face. "What's she talking about?"

"*Ma cherie.*" Andre turned toward her and smiled warmly. "We shall talk later, *mon amour*. Don't listen to this crazy woman."

The well-endowed woman stepped even closer, squinting as she saw me. "Hey, aren't you that famous girl?"

"I am."

Her jaw went slack, and a starstruck look grazed her eyes. "Cool. What are you doing here? Lining up photos with Andre?"

I scowled at Andre. "Something like that."

"Well, he's the best."

"I will be right there, *ma cherie*." Andre pointed in the distance, obviously trying to dismiss her. "Hydrate up so your face doesn't look dry."

The woman nodded and wandered to the back of the house.

"How did Cora pay you?" I continued when the woman was gone.

Andre's gaze darkened. "Cash."

I raised an eyebrow. "Did she?"

I raised my phone, the camera app open, and began snapping pictures of him.

"What are you doing?" he demanded, putting a hand in front of his face to block me.

"I'm crafting my own story to sell to the media. About the con artist posing as a photographer with a mermaid fetish."

He lowered his arms, desperation in his gaze. "No! It's not like that! I'll talk. I promise."

I paused from taking photos but kept my phone locked and loaded. "Then talk."

"Cora promised she would pay me later. She said she was going to come into some money."

Interesting. "Did she say how?"

"I have no idea. But I do know that her fingernails were dirty."

"What?" Had I heard him correctly?

"That's right. You'd think if someone was

going to pay me that much that she'd take the whole thing more seriously. But no, she came to the session looking like she'd been at the farm, and she didn't seem to care."

Siegfried had dirty hands at the party. Was there a connection? It was an idea worth exploring.

"Let's get back to the payment. What happened?" Money truly was the root of so much evil, time and time again.

"She said just that she'd pay me later. I didn't believe her. I told her I needed to be paid on the spot. That was our deal. In cash."

"The government can't track cash as easily, huh?" Tax evasion. It angered me. Probably because taxes were a thorn in my side right now. But I'd sacrificed nearly all my material possessions to make things right. I was paying my dues, and everyone else should also.

His cheeks reddened again.

I got a rush of courage and knew there was no going back. I leaned closer and made my voice deeper, more menacing. "When Cora couldn't pay you, you got mad and killed her. Am I right?"

"No! That's ridiculous. I wouldn't kill over something like this."

"I'm not sure I believe you. If you lie about one thing, who's to say you won't lie about everything." My dad had taught me that. It was called integrity, and it wasn't overrated. "I have a feeling your supposed alibi was one of your fan-club members who'd been promised the world in return for her compliance in the matter. With a little pressure, she'll cave."

"I'm not lying." He ran a hand through his hair. "Look, as Cora was leaving, she grabbed her bag and something fell out into the sand."

"What was it?"

He sighed before reaching into the pocket of his jeans and pulling out something so small I barely saw it. "This."

"What is that?" I leaned closer. It was a purple stone of some sort. Semiprecious, if I had to guess. Amethyst?

"I thought it looked valuable. I figured this could be my payment. I took it to a jeweler, and it turns out it's a purple diamond."

A purple diamond? I'd heard about them. They were expensive. Very expensive. "Why would Cora have that? She worked at the 99 Center and was struggling to make ends meet."

"I have no idea. But I considered us even."

I locked gazes with him. "Why didn't you tell the police about that? You know Cora's missing."

He glanced back at his bikini-clad friend and then stepped closer, lowering his voice. "Because

I knew how it would look. They'd think I killed her. I'm just a man trying to make a living."

Yeah, I didn't know about that.

I called Jackson as soon as I left and asked him to let the right people know. This town wasn't his jurisdiction, or I was sure he'd be here himself.

Andre may not have killed Cora, but he definitely needed to be brought in for questioning.

***

"Start over," Jackson told me as I sat in the station across from him.

He'd insisted I come in right away.

"Cora had a diamond," I told him, ticking off facts with my fingers. "It fell out of her bag, and Andre grabbed it. She was also obsessed with Nags Head Woods—more so lately, but she'd always liked it there."

"Okay, keep going."

"Meanwhile, she bought an umbrella stand. I didn't put this together at first, but I swung by 7-Eleven on the way here for a better look. The umbrella stand she bought had a little shovel thing at the end, designed to allow users to dig into the sand. But Cora could also use it to dig into dirt, if she needed to. It was something that wouldn't be too obvious if she was carrying it with her. No one would really ask questions if they saw her with it."

"I'm with you still."

"I've been told that a sea captain and his family used to live at Nags Head Woods," I continued. "When I think of sea captains, I think of people who may have encountered pirates and the like. And I know this is going to sound farfetched, but hear me out. What if one of those sea captains found some treasure and buried it?"

"How would Cora have found out about that?"

"She overheard Siegfried talking about it at one of Billy's parties. Siegfried is a historian, and he's writing a book about this area. He's been reading some old journals. I don't know the details yet—like how Cora found the diamonds before anyone else did. But she found them. And Siegfried knew that. He tracked her down, and now he has her somewhere."

Jackson leaned back. "It's an interesting theory."

"But it's a decent one."

I held my breath as I waited for his response. He couldn't argue with that fact. He just couldn't.

Finally, he nodded. "You're right. It is. We

need to find out some more information."

Satisfaction exploded inside me. "I think we should talk to Ryan, Siegfried's brother. He's always been in his sibling's shadow. Maybe he knows something he'll be willing to share."

"Let's go then."

My eyebrows shot up. "You're going to let me go with you?"

"You've got us this far. Let's see if your lead pans out."

CHAPTER 26

Ryan answered the door to the rental where he and his brother were staying. Thankfully, Jackson had been able to track down their temporary accommodations through some local realtors.

"You again." He stared at me before looking at Jackson. "And you are?"

"Detective Jackson Sullivan. Can we speak to you a minute?"

"What's this about?"

"We can do this out here, but it would be better if we went inside," Jackson said.

Ryan pulled the door back. "Sure. Come on in."

"Is your brother here?"

Ryan shook his head. "No, he's out doing more research."

Perfect! I remained quiet, just as I'd promised. But I was secretly salivating for answers.

Once we were inside, Ryan didn't offer us a

place to sit. Instead, we stood awkwardly in the living room.

"What's going on?" Ryan got right to the point. His eyes narrowed with focus.

Jackson rested his hands at his side, slipping with ease into detective mode. "Ryan, can you verify that your brother was in Raleigh last Sunday?"

"Of course he was there," Ryan said.

"For how long?"

Ryan shrugged and looked to the right, as if trying to recall details. "He did a lecture in the morning."

"So when did he come back?" Jackson continued.

He released a long breath. "I don't know. He probably got back here around two. I think it was just after I finished lunch. I didn't go with him this time since it was such a short trip."

Two. I did a mental calculation. Cora's photo session was at three. I'd found the mermaid tail at five. I'd say that was enough time to do something nefarious.

"Did your brother remain here?" Jackson asked.

Ryan's jaw locked, and he shook his head. "You're going to need to tell me more before I say anything else."

"Listen, we're trying to locate a girl that went missing from Nags Head Woods. We believe she might be connected with your brother. Time is of the essence right now."

Ryan swung his head back and forth, an incredulous look on his face. "You think Siegfried has something to do with it?"

"He's a person of interest."

"That's crazy. My brother would never do anything illegal."

"So where was he? Remember you'll be impeding a police investigation if you lie to me." Jackson's voice changed from friendly to authoritative in 5.2.

Ryan's face turned as hard as stone—until he cracked and swung his head back and forth again. "He wasn't here. But that doesn't mean he was hurting anyone or doing anything illegal."

"Where was he?" Jackson asked.

"I don't know. I didn't ask. I prefer not to be my brother's keeper, despite how it may look."

"How'd he get dirty fingernails?" I asked, breaking my stay-silent rule again.

This time Jackson didn't scowl at me, for some reason.

Ryan squeezed his eyes shut, as if guilt closed in. "I don't know. I find it's better if I don't ask. He's been researching the area, and sometimes he gets a little obsessed. He's been disappearing for hours at a time."

Jackson and I exchanged a look. It sounded like Siegfried was our guy.

Ryan ran a hand through his hair and released a guttural moan. "I hope he hasn't done anything stupid. It all started with this."

He pulled something from his pocket—a paper—and unfolded it. On the other side was a picture of a triangle with the letters *S. M.* above it and an arrow through the center. Simon Mullit. One of the people who'd lived in Nags Head Woods. A sea captain.

"What is that?" Jackson asked, staring at the paper.

"He's been reading some old journals. One of them was from the family who used to live in Nags Head Woods, and it claimed that two treasures had been buried by trees bearing this symbol. He's been obsessed with it ever since then."

Everything was starting to make sense. Cora must have found one of those treasures, and now Siegfried was desperately searching for the other.

"Where is Siegfried now?" Jackson asked, his muscles bristling so quickly that I could sense the change in the air.

"He said he was going hiking." He fidgeted and pushed his glasses higher. "What should I do?"

"Nothing," Jackson said. "Stay here. Act as if you know nothing if your brother returns."

***

Jackson and I started down the path at Nags Head Woods. I'd called Zane, who was in the middle of showing houses, and asked him if he'd ever seen that symbol that Ryan showed us. He seemed like a logical person to ask since he'd spent hours wandering these woods as a child.

And he did know.

He told us exactly how to get there.

I had a feeling this windfall Cora had mentioned was not only connected with Nags Head Woods but also with that purple diamond Andre had found. Was there also a connection with those holes Jackson and I had seen that night while searching for vandals here on the property? I thought it was a strong possibility.

"Good job with all of this, by the way," Jackson said, shining his light on the path in front of us.

"It pains you to say that, doesn't it?"

"Real life isn't like TV, Joey. In real life people

get hurt when they get nosy. You're not trained to do this, and don't tell me your acting coach taught you everything you need to know."

"How'd you know I was going to say that?"

Jackson cast me a look, and I smiled.

"You always do that, you know," he said.

"Do what?"

"Smile and make everything better."

For some reason, his words caused warmth to spread through me and joy to fill my chest. Which was ridiculous.

I remained quiet as we hiked down the narrow path, with darkness hanging around us and filling every visible inch.

"Can I ask a question?" Jackson shoved a branch out of the way.

"Of course."

"What's going on with you and Zane?"

"Me and Zane?" His question threw me off guard. "Nothing. Why?"

"You're not dating?"

I shook my head. "No, we're friends."

Even though I knew Zane wanted more. Or he thought he still did, at least.

And why did Jackson care? "Why are you asking?"

"Just making conversation."

"Oh." I paced a few more steps, my gaze

scanning the landscape around us. Was Siegfried out here? Was he watching us?

I shivered at the thought.

Even if Siegfried was here now, what did that mean for Cora? Where was she?

"Where do you think Siegfried took Cora?" I asked Jackson, careful not to trip over a root.

"I have some officers looking into his background to see if anything turns up. Hopefully they'll find something that will offer some clues."

"I hope she's okay."

"Me too."

Words seemed to lodge in my throat as I glanced over at Jackson. "Thanks for letting me come along, by the way. I know this probably wasn't your first choice, considering some of my past . . . mistakes." Was that the right word? I wasn't sure. "I'm going to prove that I'm more trustworthy. I promise."

"Things are always interesting when you're around, Joey."

I continued to shine my light on the path, hoping for some clue. If we found Siegfried, we could find Cora. I prayed she was okay.

"We should be getting close," I said. "At least, we should be if what Zane told me is correct. He said to start looking right after the railing ends. It just ended."

I stopped by a live oak. "This is the tree Zane mentioned. It has the bench also."

"This is where we go off-roading." Jackson glanced at me. "You ready for this?"

"Of course."

I immediately missed the safety of the well-marked trail, as underbrush crept around our ankles, tree roots hid just out of sight, and decomposing leaves made certain areas of the ground soft.

Jackson stayed close. That was the one good thing about all of this. I also knew that other officers were out here searching for Siegfried as well. If anything happened, we weren't alone.

Jackson placed one hand on my back. Just as a safety precaution, I reminded myself. It was so dark out here. So dark and isolated. It was the perfect place for a crime.

"Where do you see yourself ending up, Joey?" Jackson asked.

His question threw me. He was probably just trying to keep me distracted from the fears that kept wanting to surface.

"I'm not sure."

"Do you see yourself settling down somewhere away from the limelight?"

I moved closer to him as the trees squeezed

together more closely. "Those are questions I've asked myself many times. I don't know. I won't know until I have some answers about my father. He's really my only concern at the moment."

"Do you miss Hollywood?"

Again, another unexpected question. "If I were to be honest, there's something addictive about fame. It's like a drug, and you keep wanting another hit. Yet I know how unhealthy that is."

"They say that to whom much is given, much is expected. Your star power is a big responsibility."

My heart squeezed at his words. Wasn't that the revelation I'd been having lately also? I might not have worded it that way, but what he'd said was true. "I know. I want to make the most of each opportunity, but I don't want to lose myself in the process."

"That sounds smart."

Just then, Jackson's light hit a tree in the distance.

"That's it," I whispered. "That's the tree."

We rushed toward it. As Jackson shone his light on the tree, I touched the image carved into the bark decades and decades ago.

"It looks like the image Ryan showed us, doesn't it?" I asked.

"It sure does." Jackson paused. "Shall we?"

"Let's." He handed something to me. "Hold the flashlight for me."

He pulled a small camping shovel from his belt, where he'd attached it. He'd had the shovel in the back of his car, which didn't surprise me. He was a grown-up Boy Scout.

I held my breath as he dug into the dirt below the tree. A small pile formed near my feet as Jackson plowed deeper and deeper. Finally, the tip of his shovel hit something.

I sucked in a breath. A root?

Jackson got on his hands and knees and began shoving the dirt aside. A moment later, he thrust his hand into the darkness and emerged with a rusty metal box.

Our gazes connected.

I could hardly breathe as he broke the rusted lock, flipped up the latch, and pulled it open.

I knelt beside him, still holding the flashlight. A burlap bag was folded inside. Jackson gently pulled the top open. Something glistened in the depths of the fabric.

Purple diamonds.

"We found them," I said, releasing my breath. "I can't believe it. I feel like Indiana Jones."

"This was kind of fun, wasn't it?"

We shared a smile, and for a brief moment I

felt like we were partners.

"We should get out of here," Jackson said.

No sooner had the words left his lips did gunfire shatter the peace around us.

CHAPTER 27

"Get down!" Jackson jerked me closer to the ground and pulled out his gun. "Get behind the tree!"

On all fours, I scrambled across the sandy landscape. My knee hit a root, and pain pulsed through me. I ignored it and ducked behind a large oak tree. Jackson followed behind me, his gun in one hand and the treasure in the other.

"I'm calling for backup," Jackson whispered. He pushed the metal box toward me and grabbed his phone to report that shots had been fired at our location. Before he ended the conversation, he stiffened. "What? Okay. Let me know what happens."

My fingers dug into the bark of the tree as I waited for the shooter to make his next move. "Everything okay?"

Jackson shoved the phone back into his pocket, still crouched beside me with his gun raised. "Besides the fact we're being shot at?"

"Yes, besides that."

His gaze searched the distance as he peered out from behind the tree. "Detective Corbin found out that Siegfried's dad owned a hunting cabin in the area."

"What?" My voice rose in a hushed whisper.

"It's on one of those islands in the Roanoke Sound. It's really more of a shack. We have guys going out there to investigate now. It's our best lead."

Hope rose in me. Maybe Cora could be found there. Maybe all of this would be worth it and not just a lesson in futility and greed.

But there was one thing that was bothering me. What was it? The thought hovered in the back of my mind.

A twig snapped in the distance, and another bullet bit into the tree in front of us, sending wood chips raining down. The shooter had changed directions.

"We've got to keep moving," Jackson whispered. "Stay low, okay?"

"Okay."

"Hold these." He thrust the box into my hands.

This was no time to question whether or not he trusted me with the jewels. I'd do that later— once I knew we would survive this.

He grabbed my hand and tugged me into the

thick trees around us. I hugged the box to my chest, praying I didn't somehow screw this up. He'd trusted me with one task, and I didn't intend on letting him down.

He pulled me deeper into the forest, remaining low. Out of sight. Quiet.

That unknown, unable-to-put-my-finger-on-it thought continued to nag at me as we ducked through the woods. When we paused behind a tree, Jackson put a finger to his lips, indicating I should stay quiet. He needed to listen to telltale signs of our shooter, I guessed.

All I could hear was my heart furiously pounding in my ears. The Goat Man could charge me now, and I doubted I'd hear him.

That idea continued to circle in my mind. What was it? What was wrong and signaling alarm in my brain? Before the idea could emerge, footsteps charged from the darkness.

Another bullet hit wood and sent splinters raining down on us again. I sunk down, suddenly feeling exposed and like a deer being hunted.

"Shouldn't we run?" I whispered.

"We can't," Jackson said. "We're at water."

I sucked in a breath. The water. The murky swamp water. Water probably filled with leeches and snakes and other creepy crawlies.

I'd rather take my chances with a gun.

"We can't just stay here."

"Backup should be here at any time." He pressed into me—covering my body with his— as we stood behind the tree. "Just stay calm. I've got this."

Suddenly it hit me what was bothering me. I knew who really was behind this. We were looking at the wrong person. I peered out from my shelter, desperate for a glimpse of the truth.

"Jackson, I don't think Siegfried—"

My voice caught as the moonlight illuminated a figure in the distance.

And it wasn't Siegfried.

No, it was . . . Ryan.

Realization flushed through me. That was right. Ryan would have known about that family hunting cabin, but he hadn't shared the information with the police. Plus, he'd offered information on Siegfried a little too freely.

Ryan was setting his brother up to take the fall.

He paced closer toward us, his gun still raised. "There's no need for hiding. We all know what's going on here, don't we?" he said.

"You don't have to do this, Ryan," Jackson said, his gun still trained on the man, in a Mexican standoff.

"You couldn't handle your brother getting all

of the glory while you were jobless and poor, could you?" I asked.

"Just hand over the diamonds, and we can end this." Ryan paused three feet away.

"It's not that easy, Ryan," Jackson said.

I was still hyperfocused on his betrayal and feeling empowered by Jackson's presence. "You set him up. Your own flesh and blood."

"He's only ever looked out for himself. I've seen cell mates look out for each other more than he ever looked out for me."

"He discovered the diamonds through one of those journals he was reading," I said. "But you weren't about to let him find all the diamonds. You wanted a piece of the pie. You wanted the whole pie, for that matter."

He didn't deny it. "There were two burial sites. Cora found the first one. And now you just found the second one."

Even in the dark I could see the sweat across his face.

"Speaking of Cora . . . where is she?" Jackson asked.

"She's fine. She wasn't ever supposed to get involved in this." The gun trembled in Ryan's hand. This wasn't his jam, but he was going to force the issue, I realized. The money was *that* important to him.

"How did she get involved?" Jackson continued.

If we could wait him out, backup would be here soon. I hoped Ryan didn't do anything foolish in the meantime.

"Cora overheard Siegfried talking to some people at the party about those markings on the trees. He didn't mention treasure. He made it sound like they were historical markers. I knew the truth."

"And?" Jackson tugged me back behind the tree.

He'd take a bullet for me, I realized. But I'd known that before.

"And then we started talking. I thought she liked me. But my brother stepped in and asked her out. She said no. That's when I *knew* I liked her." He smirked—I could hear it in his words.

"A little competitive with your brother?" I muttered.

"Cora and I started talking about Nags Head Woods, and it turned out she had spent a lot of time exploring the grounds. I saw an opportunity. I told her that Siegfried had a silly theory about those tree markers, that pirates supposedly buried treasure there. A lot of treasure."

"You put out some bait," Jackson said.

"As soon as I said it, I could see her wheels turning. She was going to go look for herself, and I decided to follow her. She found the first set of diamonds. I couldn't believe it. And I knew she wouldn't walk away from the find, so I grabbed her."

"You tied her up at your dad's hunting cabin in the middle of an island," Jackson said.

Ryan ran a hand through his hair. "It was never supposed to go this far. But I couldn't leave town with her. People would get suspicious. They'd know I was behind this."

"Is your brother involved?" Jackson asked.

Ryan frowned, like he wanted to lie but knew there was no use. "No, he knows nothing about this. He's back at the house. I had to tie him up so he wouldn't come after me."

"There's no need to draw this out," Jackson said. "Put the gun down and let's end this."

"Why would I do that? Right now we both have a fifty-fifty chance."

"You know you're not going to shoot me," Jackson said. "It's not in you."

"Of course it is." Ryan's voice trembled.

"We just need to end this, Ryan."

"You're right. Let's end this."

A bullet rang out.

I froze. Unsure where it had come from. If I'd

been hit, for that matter. If Jackson had been hit.

Before I could react, Ryan grabbed his arm and let out a gasp. Red bled out onto his shirt. Officers rushed from the woods to apprehend him. And Jackson pulled me into his arms before I collapsed.

"You knew the officers were there, didn't you?" I asked.

"Of course I did. I wouldn't have let it go on that long otherwise."

I let out an airy, relieved laugh and let my head fall against his chest. That had been close. Too close.

Loose Lips Danny emerged from the swarm of officers and approached us. "We found Cora."

I held my breath. "And?"

Please don't let her be dead. Please.

"She's okay but is on the way to the hospital to be checked out."

Relief filled me. Good. That was all that mattered. That another life hadn't been destroyed by selfish people.

Cora was safe. Ryan had been apprehended. People had answers.

Now that those details had been settled, I had another realization.

I had to get ready for my red-eye flight to LA. Because I was leaving. Tonight.

CHAPTER 28

Despite all the excitement of the evening, I had other obligations I had to focus on right now. Hollywood.

The good news was that Cora had been found and was safe. The blood found on the mermaid tail was there because she'd cut her foot— nothing that wouldn't heal. Ryan had been arrested. The diamonds were secure. And the job was done. I could concentrate on finding my father.

Right after *Family Secrets* hit the big screen.

I glanced at my watch, realizing I had to leave for the airport in thirty minutes.

I could do this. I was *going* to do this. I'd fly solo during the press junket, and Zane would be at my side for the movie's premiere. Everything was going to be fine.

Someone knocked on my door. I glanced at my watch. Was Zane here early?

I paced to the door and opened it. To my surprised, Jackson stood there. I drew in a deep breath.

"Jackson. I wasn't expecting to see you here."

"There's something I wanted to tell you before you left for your trip."

"Oh yeah? What's that—"

Before I could finish the question, he pulled me into his arms. His lips covered mine.

I froze. Then relaxed. Then wrapped my arms around his neck.

And lost myself in the moment.

Every passionate moment. Who knew that the brooding Jackson could have so much passion inside? I wasn't going to think about it now.

Finally, he pulled away—though barely. Our faces still touched. Just our foreheads. Our arms still entangled around each other. His around my waist. Mine around his neck.

My heart raced. My lips were swollen. And my head spun. In the clouds. Hazy with emotion.

Neither of us said anything for a moment.

I ran my fingers along the hair at his neck. And his stubble. And back to his neck again.

I could still taste him. Spearmint. I wanted a replay. I wanted to run. I didn't know what I wanted.

I was in so much trouble.

I cleared my throat and tried to pull myself together. "Do you . . . want to come inside?"

Jackson didn't say anything, so I opened the door. Still facing each other, we gravitated inside, almost as if neither of us ever wanted to let go. Jackson shut the door behind us.

This was the time we should talk. Where I should ask questions. Where I needed to put my head before my heart.

I forced myself to step back. I tried to speak, but my tongue didn't cooperate. All I could think about was that kiss. That very unexpected yet delightful kiss.

Thankfully, Jackson said something. His voice was hoarse with emotion. "You drive me crazy, Joey."

Okay, not really what I wanted to hear. "I suspected that."

He grinned, his fingers pressing into my skin as he pulled me closer. "Crazy in a good way. I can't stop thinking about you. I wasn't looking for any of this."

"Any of what?"

He shook his head, a dark emotion coming over him. I knew. He wasn't looking for a relationship. Not after Claire.

I really had nothing to say, even though I

knew I should.

Instead I reached up, and I kissed him this time. Softly—but only for a couple of seconds. Then all of that pent-up passion unleashed again. And I felt like I could kiss him and keep kissing him and never walk away from this moment.

When we pulled away, we were breathless. I could feel his heart. And reality hit me.

"I'm a mess, Jackson," I whispered.

"What do you mean?"

"I mean, I make messes out of everything I touch."

"I don't believe that."

"You should. I don't want to make a mess of you too." I stepped back, regret lodging itself in my chest.

Jackson didn't let go though. "Joey . . ."

"You deserve someone who's . . ." *Who's what, Joey?* "Who's . . . unblemished."

"There's no one who exists like that."

I licked my lips. "Well, there are people who are closer than I am."

"Joey . . ."

I rested my hand on his chest, still drawn to him even though I knew I shouldn't be. I needed to cut this off now before we both got in over our heads. Jackson might not think it now, but he deserved better than me. I didn't even know if I could ever truly trust a man again. Nor was I sure I was ready to try.

"I have to go, Jackson. I have to catch a flight to LA."

He pushed a stray hair behind my ear. "Think about it? Think about us, okay?"

I nibbled on my still-swollen lip. "I'm pretty sure I won't be able to stop. But . . ." There was so much I needed to tell him. I needed to slash his hopes that we could ever make it.

"No buts," he said. "Just think about it."

I thought he might kiss me again. Instead, he wrapped his arms around my shoulders and pulled me toward him. He kissed the top of my head.

And in an instant, I felt safe. Loved. Like I never wanted him to let me go.

But I was in no position to keep holding on. Not if I wanted to be fair to him. "Jackson—"

Someone knocked on the door. "Joey, you ready to go?"

Zane, I realized.

I stepped away from Jackson, feeling at odds with myself and the future and . . . everything else.

"We'll talk when you get back," Jackson said.

I nodded, wishing he didn't have to leave. That I didn't have to leave. Happy he had to leave. Happy I had to leave.

Confused. Mostly, I was confused.

I was like Sybil from the movie, with multiple personalities warring inside me.

I opened the door, and sure enough, Zane stood there. His gaze darted back and forth from me and Jackson, as if he sensed he'd interrupted something. Jackson nodded and stepped out with a wave.

He gave me one last heated glance. "Have a good trip, Joey."

"Thanks." My voice cracked as I watched him walk away.

"Everything okay?" Zane asked, squeezing my arm.

I nodded a little too quickly, desperately hoping I didn't have any telltale signs of our kiss. Obviously swollen lips. Smeared makeup. Tousled hair. "Yeah, of course. It's good. Great. You ready to go?"

He was driving me to the airport up in Norfolk, Virginia. He'd meet me in seven days, after my press junket, for the premiere. And I knew we were going to have a great time together. Zane was made for stuff like this and would easily incorporate into my Hollywood life.

But it wouldn't all be fun and games. Because Eric would be there also. Nothing in my life was simple. Especially when it came to men.

Zane thrust out his hand. "By the way, I found this in the mailbox. I think it was intended for you."

My lungs tightened as I took the paper from him. I'd recognize the shape of the paper anywhere. My stalkers. This was what nearly every message they'd sent me had looked like.

My fingers trembled as I unfolded it. Sure enough, familiar scrawl decorated the inside. I held my breath as I read the words there.

> *Kudos on another job well done. We'd hate to see this end. Just for incentive in the future, we have an offer: For every mystery you solve from here on out, we'll give you one clue about your father. Good luck. Ready, set, go!*

###

Coming Next:

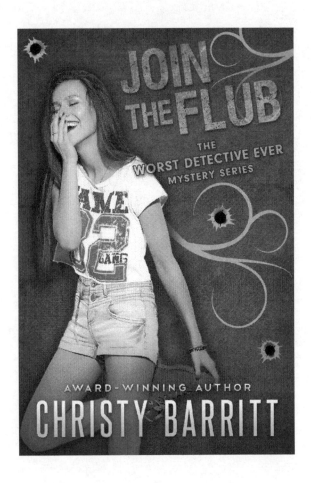

Complete Book List

Squeaky Clean Mysteries

Hazardous Duty

Suspicious Minds

It Came Upon a Midnight Crime

Organized Grime

Dirty Deeds

The Scum of All Fears

To Love, Honor, and perish

Mucky Streak

While You Were Sweeping (A Riley Thomas Novella)

Foul Play

Broom and Gloom

Dust and Obey

Thrill Squeaker

Swept Away

Cunning Attractions

Clean Getaway (coming soon)

Holly Anna Paladin Mysteries

Random Acts of Murder

Random Acts of Deceit

Random Acts of Malice

Random Acts of Scrooge

Random Acts of Greed

Random Acts of Fraud (coming soon)

The Sierra Files
Pounced
Hunted
Pranced
Rattled
Caged (coming soon)

The Worst Detective Ever
Ready to Fumble
Reign of Error
Safety in Blunders
Join the Flub (coming soon)
Blooper Freak (coming soon)

Suburban Sleuth Mysteries
Death of a Couch Potato's Wife

Cape Thomas Series
Dubiosity
Disillusioned
Distorted (coming soon)

Carolina Moon Series
Home Before Dark
Gone By Dark
Wait Until Dark

Light the Dark

Tween Novels
The Curtain Call Caper
The Disappearing Dog Dilemma
The Bungled Bike Burglaries

Stand Alone Novels
The Trouble With Perfect
The Good Girl

Non Fiction Titles
The Novel In Me
Changed

ABOUT THE AUTHOR

USA Today has called Christy Barritt's books "scary, funny, passionate, and quirky."

Christy writes both mystery and romantic suspense novels that are clean with underlying messages of faith. Her books have won the Daphne du Maurier Award for Excellence in Suspense and Mystery, have been twice nominated for the Romantic Times Reviewers' Choice Award, and have finaled for both a Carol Award and *Foreword Reviews* magazine's Book of the Year.

She is married to her prince charming, a man who thinks she's hilarious—but only when she's not trying to be. Christy is a self-proclaimed klutz, an avid music lover who's known for spontaneously bursting into song, and a road-trip aficionado.

When she's not working or spending time with her family, she enjoys singing, playing the guitar, and exploring small, unsuspecting towns where people have no idea how accident prone she is.

Find Christy online at: